VAN BUREN
DECATUR, MICHIGAN 49045

P9-DDZ-775

DISCARDED

The Hatwearer's Lesson

ALSO BY YOLANDA JOE

This Just In
Bebe's By Golly Wow!
He Say, She Say
Falling Leaves of Ivy

The Hatwearer's Lesson

Yolanda Joe

DUTTON

Joe

DUTTON
Published by the Penguin Group
Penguin Putnam Inc., 375 Hudson Street, New York, New York 10014, U.S.A.
Penguin Books Ltd, 80 Strand, London WC2R 0RL, England
Penguin Books Australia Ltd, 250 Camberwell Road, Camberwell, Victoria 3124, Australia
Penguin Books Canada Ltd, 10 Alcorn Avenue, Toronto, Ontario, Canada M4V 3B2
Penguin Books (N.Z.) Ltd, Cnr Rosedale and Airborne Roads,
Albany, Auckland 1310, New Zealand

Penguin Books Ltd, Registered Offices: Harmondsworth, Middlesex, England

Published by Dutton, a member of Penguin Putnam Inc.

First printing, March 2003
1 3 5 7 9 10 8 6 4 2

Copyright © Yolanda Joe, 2003
All rights reserved

 REGISTERED TRADEMARK—MARCA REGISTRADA

LIBRARY OF CONGRESS CATALOGING-IN-PUBLICATION DATA:

Joe, Yolanda.
The hatwearer's lesson / by Yolanda Joe.
p. cm.
ISBN 0-525-94716-7
1. African American families—Fiction. 2. African American women—Fiction.
3. Grandparent and child—Fiction. 4. Women lawyers—Fiction. 5. Grandmothers—Fiction.
6. Arkansas—Fiction. I. Title.

PS3560.O242 H3 2003
813'.54—dc21   2002037900

Printed in the United States of America
Set in Galliard
Designed by Leonard Telesca

PUBLISHER'S NOTE

This is a work of fiction. Names, characters, places, and incidents either are the products of the author's imagination or are used fictitiously, and any resemblance to actual persons, living or dead, business establishments, events, or locales is entirely coincidental.

Without limiting the rights under copyright reserved above, no part of this publication may be reproduced, stored in or introduced into a retrieval system, or transmitted, in any form, or by any means (electronic, mechanical, photocopying, recording, or otherwise), without the prior written permission of both the copyright owner and the above publisher of this book.

The scanning, uploading, and distribution of this book via the Internet or via any other means without the permission of the publisher is illegal and punishable by law. Please purchase only authorized electronic editions, and do not participate in or encourage electronic piracy of copyrighted materials. Your support of the author's rights is appreciated.

This book is printed on acid-free paper.

3-03
B+T

For my grandmothers: Bernice Barnett and Clara Joe.
I'd like to imagine that when they each got to heaven
the angels said, "Like that hat, girl."

Thanks

A writer is not a writer without a great team working with her.

First and foremost, thanks to my agent, Victoria, who is smart, funny, caring, and more important, a friend.

To my editor, Laurie, who helped me shape this book and make it the compassionate piece it is today: You are fabulous to work with and I appreciate everything you do.

To Stephanie, who is Laurie's right hand and my left—whenever I need something she's on the case: Your future in the biz is filled with bright lights, kiddo.

And finally, words on a page cannot properly thank people who have done so much for me; only prayers from the heart will really do. I'll keep you in my prayers, guys. God bless.

PROLOGUE

The Bad Sign

Grandma Ollie broke down her Sunday hat the way the setting sun puts a crease in the evening sky. She had perfected the technique with the help of her big sister, Lula, back in Arkansas, some sixty years ago; a sister she still grieved for to this very day.

Breaking down a hat is a family trait just like blue veins beneath red-boned skin, sultry eyes, or book smarts. Grandma Ollie had been determined to pass perfection of that trait on to her granddaughter, Terri.

When Terri was fourteen they took a road trip from the city to the South to visit some kin. Southern girls loved to wear their Sunday hats. The hats, draped with lace, blossoming with color, were crowns that granted the wearer sovereignty wherever she went.

Grandma Ollie introduced her granddaughter, Terri, to

the power of the brim. She showed Terri how to press the fold, tilt the hat forward, drop the brim real low. It gave off a special attitude and left the wearer, well, might as well g'on and tell the truth, damn near legally blind.

"How am I supposed to look where I'm going?" Terri had asked in the loft of a frame house in Collingswood, Arkansas.

"Chile-chile!" Grandma Ollie sucked wind. "The only *looking* you need to worry about is looking *good.*"

"Well, can't I *see some?*"

"How much?"

"More than Stevie Wonder."

Grandma Ollie tilted the hat to the right. "Now there. Use your left eye."

"What am I? A sewing needle? I need more than one eye!"

And hadn't Terri been right? Sure enough when she came prancing across the room that day to go to church she didn't see the cellar hatch open. What did a city girl know about cellars?

Terri stepped where the floor ought to have been and fell straight down to where she had no business being. Luckily there was a pile of old clothes for her to land on in the root cellar.

Both of Terri's shoes flipped crossways on the tips of her toes. Her skinny legs folded together at the knees. Terri's hat sailed off. A patch of hair stood up dry as a wick. The girl was dangerous. Her body was sign language for "T-N-T."

Grandma Ollie hollered down from the great room upstairs, "Hello down there. You all right?"

"Yeah."

"Sure?"

"Yeah."

"Well, since you down there, bring up one of them jugs."

Grandma Ollie chuckled at the memory now as she continued to examine herself in the mirror. This was her favorite hat for two reasons. One, it was a Mother's Day present from Terri, the child she raised who had been both blessed and cursed with her ways.

And two, because the hat was flaming violet, the color of Grandma Ollie's early days of womanhood, and had a band wide and unbroken like her nerve, and a feather that flared when it had a mind to, like her temper.

Grandma Ollie savored her reflection in the mirror.

She remembered how her hair once flowed red and wild. How her hips once swayed sturdy and smooth like a rocking chair. How when she used to laugh, her cheeks had the roll, the sparkle, and the puff of soapy dishwater. How she danced and her feet went exactly where they should without tiring.

Grandma Ollie knew she had been swindled. She thought, There should be a law against it; wonder what that low-down dirty dog Time has done with all my stuff?

Time ripped her off. Traded her black hair color out of a bottle, pain reliever in a tube, blush in a compact, and a cane she folded up and slid under the bed at night.

Grandma Ollie figured she'd been cheated worse than the Indians who swapped Manhattan for a bag of beads. At least they got some jewelry out of the deal. Yes Lord.

Grandma Ollie tweaked the hat until it defied gravity. She investigated herself from tip to top. Her lilac dress, laced around the rolled collar, fit to form. Grandma Ollie was pleased with herself: "You together."

She grabbed her folding cane off the bed and snapped it open, then began the long struggling walk to the front room. Her bad hip was getting worse, but she chose not to tell anyone. Especially Terri.

Grandma Ollie plopped down in her double-cushioned chair by the window. She would wait patiently for her ride to Wednesday night prayer meeting. She snapped her white gloves against flushed palms before opening up her Bible. The first page read, "Given To:" Her father had written in his fifth-grade hand her name and the date . . .

Olivia Anderson. June 4, 1935.

She flipped to the page entitled, "Marriages." There, written in her own hand was . . .

Olivia Anderson engaged to Wesley Strong on April 19, 1943.

Beneath that she'd written . . .

Married August 28, 1944, 'til death do them part.

Grandma Ollie lovingly traced Wesley's name with her fingertips. She missed her husband of more than half a century. She'd taken his death hard. Had it not been for Terri, no telling what she might have done.

Thinking of Terri! Lord have mercy. Terri and that handsome boy Derek had gotten engaged more than a month ago. And Grandma Ollie hadn't set it down. Where was her mind?

Grandma Ollie took a pen out of the cup holder on the windowsill and began to write . . .

Terri Mills engaged to . . .

Then the brand-new pen up and died; ran completely out of ink. Got dry as graveyard bones. Grandma Ollie couldn't write the boy's name down in the Bible. This was sho' nuff a sign.

A sign can be a dream or an unusual gesture by a person or by nature. Life is full of signs. Grandma Ollie was one of the few who could read them.

"Something's *wrong-wrong*," she said as her eyes scissored shut.

Grandma Ollie closed the Bible and started to pray. She did not pray for herself, but for her heart up north—her granddaughter, Terri, whose life had almost been lost *twice* in two rivers.

Chapter 1

The first river was in the womb.

Terri was the child of Grandma Ollie's daughter, Magpie. She was given the nickname Magpie in the little country town of Collingswood, Arkansas.

During the great migration, colored folks gathered up all things held dear and packed them into big, bulky cardboard suitcases.

Happily, they boarded trains and jilted the Jim Crow South, leaving it behind them like the stiff, black rails that carried them north.

But they carried with them country ways, still loving their floral aprons, white shoes after Labor Day, and don't you know, nicknames like Skeeter, June Bug, and Magpie.

Magpie had fallen in love with James. He was a Collingswood boy. The children were as inseparable as back and front.

Magpie and James began their lives together toddling along Arkansas's dirt roads. They were thick as angels. The sun would toast their necks and the breeze would bounce their giggles over yonder the way little children skip pebbles cross-stream.

When both Magpie and James were only five years old, James's family and Grandma Ollie and her husband, Wesley, brought their families north. Together, the two families thought they could make it.

New York was the initial destination—Harlem to be exact; the city in the colored picture shows where all the women wore fur coats and all the men had good hair.

But the train ride had been so tiring that they stopped in Chicago instead; a colored porter swore up and down to them that Bill "Bojangles" Robinson and other famous folk like that loved to visit the Windy City too.

As time passed, the children got fly, shame of their starched country clothes and out-of-style shoes. They picked up slang as teenagers. Magpie's sweaters got tighter and James's hats got to hanging off his ear.

The *cooler* they got, the *wilder* they got.

Magpie became pregnant with James's baby. Did she slow down? No. She and James still followed the light; the light of the marquee that glowed in front of the trendy colored nightclubs.

It was inside one of these nightclubs that pain crippled Magpie. She doubled over. Everyone assumed she must have had too much to drink again—like James, who was passed out in a back booth.

But a river had grown inside of her—and Magpie hadn't even noticed it, this being her seventh month. Drinking hard liquor and hardly any water, her stomach had ballooned. Unhappy with James and the life they were living, she had been depressed and drank more. And the river of her discontentment grew and grew.

It was that river that was raging all around Terri in the womb. Grinding in her ears in the womb. Tickling the bottoms of her delicate feet. Washing against her stretched, pained skin. Battering against her developing spirit.

That river had begun to drown Terri, the unborn child.

How had Magpie known? Because of the sign. Grandma Ollie had read it, not two weeks before. She watched as a nest of birds made a home on a branch outside the kitchen window of their tiny cold-water flat.

Magpie was sitting there, eating jam and biscuits, catching a breeze, when the birds, startled by the sound of a train whistle, bolted. Water, nestled among the leaves from a late night rain, splattered Magpie's cotton top and ran down her stomach like a river.

Tears formed in Grandma Ollie's eyes as she watched that river crawl along the girl's stomach, which now looked huge and purplish beneath the cotton cloth, and she knew.

"Magpie, I've got a bad feeling. Stay home these next few nights, please."

Magpie chuckled, a firm, tart laugh; admonishing Grandma Ollie for hoarding her country ways. Magpie wasn't near due—only seven months and she was big—from cola drinks and nothing more.

But it was the river. Magpie staggered forward in the nightclub, speechless from fear, feet driven to make it back to her mother's door, through desolate streets, slick and awash with mist from a sky that couldn't decide whether to merely pout or cry outright.

Let me make it, Magpie prayed. Let me make it.

Only her mother's hands could pull this baby from the river. She could see that now . . . not like before when Magpie had been blind from anger at poverty, at James's philandering, at the shattered promises of the world.

No need for a hospital. Doctors? Who? Not them. She wanted to save this baby, and only her hatwearing, signreading mother could. But would her mother be able to save her?

"My child, my child," Grandma Ollie said when Magpie fell at her feet not more than five steps into the front room.

The hardwood floor cried out as her body jerked uncontrollably. "Save the baby, Mama, save the baby."

And she took her daughter in her arms, pulled her up in front of her, like they were rowing a boat, and together they began to ride the river.

The prayers that leapt from Grandma Ollie's lips were spoken in some sacred tongue that graced only the mouths of mothers in distress and could be understood only by the ears of angels.

Grandma Ollie just swayed and rubbed Magpie's stomach, the river raging beneath the layers of skin, threatening to drown her unborn grandchild.

And she rubbed. . . .

Her thoughts traveled over miles of memory, some hers, some divine from her mother's spirit, others belonging to ancestors she'd only seen pictures of . . . They came to mind and helped Grandma Ollie now as she prayed and rubbed.

The river broke and Grandma Ollie knelt before the rush of water, told Magpie to push, to push her baby forward, and she would pull, save her from this raging river. And through all this Terri came into the world and her mother Magpie left it.

Terri's first sight was her mother's spirit leaving, and that made her forever long for something that was missing. So she was born with a soul that opened up inside of her like a web. It was complicated and fragile, invisible to the naked eye of others until they got close enough to get caught up in it. Terri would play with her toes in her handmade crib and stop, suddenly, little brow wrinkling, unsure of what, but knowing something was missing.

When Terri was seven, her father, James, had agonized enough over his guilt about Magpie's death; it filled his shoes like itchy feet and made it hard for him to stay in one place. So one day he told Terri that he loved her very much.

And then James left.

Terri waited and waited, looking out of the window, waiting for her daddy. She watched the sun go down and the moon come out. But he never returned.

So Terri always seemed to be waiting, waiting for the return of things. Grandma Ollie raised her, loved her like her own, of course, because she had pulled Terri from the river.

But Terri would be hesitant to fully trust any other love

that was shown to her; skeptical, she thought that somehow there was something missing from it or that if pure, it would mysteriously vanish.

Terri began to collect things, material things, dolls, toys, things to help fill the void: the void of what was missing and what had left. Never was she stingy with the things that she collected for comfort, but still she needed them, felt secure with them.

Grandma Ollie had feared that at some point Terri would begin to covet material things instead of merely appreciating them. So she made sure that many of the things were somehow earned, through extra chores or academic achievements. And as Terri's childhood turned into adolescence, and her adolescence turned into adulthood, Grandma Ollie's fear shifted.

She knew that somehow, some way, Terri would have to learn to accept and trust the love of others, but how could she help that learning begin?

Chapter 2

A failure in Terri and Derek's love odyssey would be the catalyst.

Terri and her fiancé, Derek, were dream merchants. They took the contents of their ancestors' hope chest and turned them into millennium silver and gold—*that being power and prestige.*

Terri graduated summa cum laude from Duke, studied abroad in France, made law review at Harvard, had six job offers upon graduation. She selected a five-star firm with one female partner and no African-Americans.

Terri wanted to stand out in more ways than one.

The pin-striped partners of privilege thought Terri would be the spook who sat by the door, glad to collect a six-figure salary and forget all about causes, the way their wives overlooked sale coupons in the Sunday newspaper.

But, you see, they didn't know how Terri was raised. Grandma Ollie had shared with Terri her people's collective dream, their iridescent hope. From the parched soil where sharecroppers toiled, from schoolhouse doors blocked by barking dogs, from the shallow graves of slain civil rights workers . . .

A dream. A hope.

From Grandma Ollie's generation to the next sprang up a collective dream that their children would have more choices than to labor by hand, that their talents would be nurtured, that their achievements would be recognized, that they would vote without fear and compete without reprisals.

In short, that little colored children who could—*would* soar.

Terri decided to get her wings in law. She made that choice after struggling through parts of her history book, unable to understand how slavery so easily became the law of the land. Grandma Ollie was unsure of how to explain it to Terri until the two of them went one day to the grocery store to get a roast for Sunday dinner.

The man behind the counter had written out the prices on a big board. He got the meat, weighed it, and then wrote down how much it would cost. There was no haggling. Everyone saw what was what, and that was that. Grandma Ollie explained that it was in that same way that men wrote down the rules of slavery years ago and everyone accepted it.

Terri learned that it was the law that had determined the value of an entire people, three-fifths a human being, like the butcher who priced meat at the corner store. She also learned that it was the law that had helped to change things for the better.

So Terri vowed to be the best lawyer that she could. She went to that high-powered firm on a mission. Terri wowed them with her smarts, dazzled them with her impeccable dress, and talked circles around them on many occasions without them even knowing it.

By the time they figured it out, Terri had gotten two black male attorneys hired and one Hispanic woman. The partners had been properly played for the better good—except they didn't want to be good. So the buzz was that come *partner-picking time* it might be *cotton-picking time* for Terri.

So Terri broke camp and felt good about it. She didn't want to languish in a windchill tower overlooking Chicago's Lake Michigan anyway.

Terri wanted to wet her beak in politics.

She took a job with the city, putting out fires. Contract fires. Multimillion-dollar contracts. If it involved megabucks, Terri was the dealer. She did her homework and yours too. She bluffed without blinking.

Well, except for that one time.

Terri had a meeting with a construction company that had a megabucks deal to repair roads. Their work was shabby, not to mention the fact that the company had fallen from favor with the political powerhouses. So the city wanted to blow up the contract.

The construction company wanted to sue.

Terri and her legal brain trust squared off against the

company's legal think tank. They snapped and snarled. Terri bit and tore. She had them off balance, backpedaling.

"In addition to the difficulty we are having with your workmanship," Terri said in mock amazement, "I see that you do not have any women or minorities on your upper management team."

"Well, we've been working on that," they answered.

"Oh, did you gentlemen think the term 'with all deliberate speed' referred only to pouring concrete?"

The next meeting, Terri blinked.

There was a new negotiator at the table. He was tall and willowy with chestnut brown skin, large eyes, and a piano-keys smile. Most of his features were average but his charisma was not. He oozed control. Finesse.

Blink. Blink.

Terri felt her insides stir. Grandma Ollie had been tearing her up with that switch in her voice. *When you gonna meet somebody? Don't you want to have children? It don't pay for a woman to grow old alone.*

Grandma Ollie could stress out a light pole.

Derek Houser was the man's name. He was a Howard graduate and in the top ten percent of his Yale Law School class. He'd worked for the state in several positions but decided three years ago to start his own business.

The construction company was bringing him on board as a paid legal consultant. Terri had baited the hook for them and Derek was the catch. Of course, after this legal matter was settled, they'd throw him back.

But Terri wouldn't.

She allowed Derek to take her to dinner when the negotiations were over. That was the beginning of things that grow.

In the fall, seeds are shed and find their place in the soil. Some languish there, a possibility never developed, while others get the nourishment they need and flourish openly in front of the world.

Such was the relationship between Terri and Derek.

They were a power couple. They had credentials and cash. They had talent and used it to get all the toys. Terri had more than thirty pairs of designer shoes in her closet. There was a BMW convertible in the garage of Terri's Hyde Park condo overlooking the lakefront.

Derek had a Jaguar XJ6 in the driveway of his Lincoln Park town house. He loved custom-made suits, traveled to Italy to buy material once a year. Derek had a style all his own—too B-boy for Brooks Brothers yet too good-old-boy for *GQ*.

And he knew how to pull it off too.

Derek walked proud, aggressively, yet his mannerisms were always calm and inviting. He looked prominent . . . headed somewhere important. Derek was so bad that when he stood on North Michigan Avenue and threw up his hand, *two cabs* stopped.

Derek made it a point to smoke cigars in the back room with the big boys. He taught Terri how to play golf; took her to play with some of the city's heavy hitters of politics. Derek shared his contacts with Terri, grooming her as he was groomed. Usually neither the brothers nor the good old boys would include a sister in their frats. So Terri knew all too well how generous this was of Derek, and it deeply endeared him to her. Together they networked toward success.

Derek and Terri went to fund-raisers and political dinners, charity galas, even an event called the Who's Who Chicago Walk-a-thon.

Moving and shaking.

But Terri and Derek knew how to mix it up too. They were at the head table for the sorority scholarship dinner. They were in the outfield for the coed softball game at the fraternity's annual picnic. They had it going on so tough that you wanted to be them.

Either one of them, didn't matter which one.

Terri loved how people whispered when they walked into a room. Derek loved how Terri looked on his arm, her ease with meeting new people—well read, never at a loss to contribute to any conversation.

Separately they were going places. Together they seemed already there.

Derek flirted with women and joked with men. He was irresistible—sometimes too irresistible for Terri's taste. She had a jealous streak but tried to keep it in check.

But Derek liked to mess with Terri's mind just so she'd blow up at him. Derek mischievously enjoyed the physical steam it took for them to make up later.

One night Terri went and sulked at the bar after Derek meandered from one pretty girl to another at a black MBA mixer. One woman in particular really made Terri angry. She just happened to be a secretary at her best friend's firm. Zelda was the woman's name.

Zelda came to all the after-work mixers, NAACP dinners, and such, but always managed to master a cheap appearance.

Her clothes were notoriously too bright or too tight. Zelda had a body to die for—tiny waist, round hips, arms of steel, but way too much behind.

Grandma Ollie used to say, *Too much behind may mean a weak mind.*

That night Derek flirted a little too far. Putting way too much bounce and hip in his dance moves, rubbing up against all that behind. When Derek spun around, it looked like he had a hole in his pocket and a roll of quarters had slipped through. And Zelda? She was grinning enough teeth to star in an Ultra Brite toothpaste commercial.

Terri was determined not to show her emotions. Derek came up behind her at the bar. She was wolfing down cherry after cherry, frantically stirring a drink.

He whispered, "I thought you lost your cherry a long time ago."

Terri chewed then swallowed. "Well, when you get over thirty it comes back. Then you get to lose it all over again."

Losing the phony vibe of the club scene, Terri and Derek left and later found themselves completely naked, sitting a few inches apart, locked in a visual embrace. Not a bit shy, they let their eyes stroke each other's most inviting points of passion.

Derek's vision circled Terri's full lips, hot brown, and ready to scorch the tongue. He let his next sight be the slide of her neck, which he planned to let his fingertips ride with abandon. What fetched his gaze now was the roll of her thighs, taut as they rested against the edge of the bed.

Meanwhile Terri took a gander at Derek's squared shoulders, stretched tight with coiled muscles set to react to the woman passionately poised next to him. Terri's gaze left the top half of his luscious body and meandered down to his sexy stomach, which made her smile as she imagined the steamy kisses she planned on placing there.

The couple wantonly soaked up all the sex appeal that leapt from their separated bodies. They appreciated the draw of man to woman. This little game was all Terri's idea. It was designed so that when they did finally touch, Derek was sufficiently stirred up and Terri had sensually sized him up.

Grandma Ollie would size up Derek's character in another manner. He went with Terri to visit her one Thanksgiving. At the end of the holiday, Grandma Ollie pronounced her evaluation. "As smooth talking as you are, Derek-boy, good thing you're going into politics. Otherwise you'd be a crook."

Derek thought it was funny. Terri got upset.

Grandma Ollie told her, "I'm over seventy years old. I'll say what I wanna say. And all of it will likely be true. He's all right, Terri. If you like it, I love it."

Shortly after the couple's return to Chicago, Derek and Terri were at his place one night. The curtains in his bedroom were drawn tight. The light was off. It was completely dark.

Derek hugged Terri close. "Wanna win a prize?" he asked.

"Sure," she said, enjoying the lush smell of cologne on Derek's neck.

"Answer this question."

"Hmmmm-huh," she purred, kissing him passionately.

"What town did the Flintstones live in?"

"Bedrock."

"That's right!" Derek said, turning on the light.

There was the bed.

And on the bed was a rock.

It was the biggest, most beautiful diamond Terri had ever seen. She gasped, *"Oh baby, you know how to hurt a sister right."*

"Marry me and we'll show the world what's what, girl. Say yes, Terri."

And she did.

That's why Grandma Ollie's call disturbed her so.

"Terri, chile, I swear, something is wrong. I couldn't write that boy's name down for nothing in the world."

"Grandma Ollie, that sign stuff is so old-fashioned. Maybe you just bought a bad pen, what about that?"

"Listen here, I can read signs better than I can read my own name. Something is wrong. Tell Derek to watch his self. And you watch yourself too."

Terri hated it when Grandma Ollie saw a sign. It made her nervous. Much as she hated to admit it, and much as Grandma Ollie liked to let her know it, more often than not, she'd be dead on about those signs.

Was Derek in danger? He traveled a great deal. In fact, Terri was driving him to the airport this evening. She was going to use Derek's car because hers was being worked on.

The day crept along, with Grandma Ollie's warning hanging over Terri's head as heavy as the dark clouds that filled the sky. By that evening Grandma Ollie's warning and the clouds had both swelled and burst, filling the air around the couple with foreboding.

"Derek, I don't like this weather," Terri said as they drove to the airport in the rain. "You should change your flight. Why don't you go tomorrow morning sometime?"

"Baby, I don't want to miss a second of this conference. Heavyweights from the Democratic National Party will be there. I need to be on the case from the opening breakfast on, networking my butt off."

Terri bit her lip as she pulled into the passenger drop-off lane.

"You worry too much," Derek said, and kissed her neck before grabbing his Louis Vuitton suit bag off the backseat. "Don't forget to let the cable guy in for me tomorrow so he can rewire my den. Love you, bye!"

Terri tried valiantly to resist worrying about Derek. But she just kept hearing Grandma Ollie's voice . . .

Terri, chile, I swear, something is wrong. I couldn't write that boy's name down for nothing in the world.

Raindrops pounded against the windshield. Terri turned on the radio and tried to think of other things.

Something is wrong. Tell Derek to watch his self. And you watch yourself too.

Suddenly a horn blared from her right. Terri's heart leapt, sending pain shooting from her chest up through her ears. She swerved to the right and the two cars just missed careening into each other.

Terri managed to straighten out the Jaguar. The thunder clapping in the gray sky seemed indistinguishable from the clatter of her frightened heart.

Terri pulled over to the side of the road. It took her ten minutes to calm down. Grandma Ollie and her signs had Terri coming and going.

Who believes in signs and such these days? Wasn't she a contemporary black woman? Wasn't she a lawyer and didn't lawyers only deal in facts?

The hard swerve had sparked disarray inside the car. Terri reached over and righted the cup holder and began picking up the change and pens, some of which had rolled under the seat.

Her hand sank a bit in the Jaguar's plush carpet. "Got it!" she said finding the last pen, but she also grabbed a piece of paper.

It was a white stub from an airline ticket. Terri was about to toss it away when she noticed that it read, "D. Houser. Cancún, Mexico."

When did Derek go to Cancún? She looked at the date from two weeks ago. He'd told Terri that he was going to Florida for a three-day weekend to play golf with his brother.

Terri ran her hand underneath the car seat again. This time she found a stubby eyebrow pencil. Light brown. Maybelline. Not her color. Not her brand.

The strange ticket and eyebrow pencil rocked Terri to the core. She could neither erase the evidence nor rationalize it. Then the river inside her began to rage. The waters rose and began to spill out of Terri's eyes as she drove home. The river ran freely for hours, and just when Terri thought she might go completely under, she reached out to Grandma Ollie.

Chapter 3

Grandma Ollie listened as Terri's northern heart wept over the phone. "Shoosh now, Terri," she murmured. "Shoosh now."

The call had awakened her in the middle of the night. "Didn't I tell you something was wrong? I need to get me one of those pricey one-eight-hundred-who-ja-mah-call-its. Make more money than Oprah."

Terri sobbed.

"Baby don't cry. You know Grandma knows."

"I mean I put my trust in Derek. And now I find out that I've been bamboozled. Betrayed. Played. How could Derek just trip out on me like that?"

"Terri, I don't know what's on the minds of these mens sometimes. I swear I don't."

"I'm gonna call Derek right now, wake him up and cuss him to kingdom come."

"No you don't, chile. That ain't the way. You need to have your stuff together. You need to have things in order."

"In order how?"

"Terri, you need to know exactly what you're going to say. You need to be looking out of sight too—face-to-face, calm and cool, not all flushed and hysterical. Confront him with the facts, and then cuss him in a low voice. That'll scare the living stew out of him. Do you know who he's been two-timing you with?"

"Yes," Terri sniffed hard, picturing Zelda in the club grinding on Derek. "And I'm going to get that heifer too. It's her fault."

"No ma'am; didn't nobody make Derek do wrong but Derek."

Terri listened but knew she was going to get Zelda. She didn't care what Grandma Ollie said.

"Terri, you still gonna let the cable people into that boy's place tomorrow afternoon?"

"Oh yeah. And I'm gonna do some snooping too while I'm there. I would go tonight but I'm too upset. I need to rest. I've got to be on point tomorrow."

"Now you talking like you some kin to me."

What Terri didn't tell Grandma Ollie was that first thing in the morning she was going to jam up Zelda. She called her best friend, Niecy, who was a partner at Zelda's firm.

"Do me a favor. Jam Zelda up whenever you can."

"Your timing is superb, girl. She just applied for a training program here. We pick one secretary to be trained as a paralegal. Zelda had a very good interview."

Terri hesitated, knowing Grandma Ollie would disapprove.

"Terri, you there?"

"Yeah."

"She has the best shot at the job."

"Well now she's shot down."

That afternoon Terri let the cable man into Derek's town house. He was cute and tried to flirt. She was not in the mood. Terri let him know that this was her fiancé's place. The cable man dropped the mack-daddy routine and got right to work.

So did Terri.

She snooped old-school style; like Mannix, Kojak, Police Woman, and Christie Love. She went through drawers. She looked under the bed and in the linen closet.

Terri was in the master bedroom when she looked up and the cable man was standing in the doorway. Startled, Terri nearly dropped the wooden drawer on her toes.

The young man, around thirty years old, tall, light-skinned, bucktoothed, and buff, gave Terri a disapproving look. "Y'all sistahs are a trip."

Terri felt judged. Angrily she asked, "Whadaya need?"

"I just wanted to know if your fiancé would mind if I did some drilling, to run the wire through the wall. It'll look better but it'll leave a medium-sized hole."

Terri shrugged in a very irritated manner: *So?*

When the cable man disappeared from the doorway, she sat down on the bed and fought the urge to cry. She picked up the phone and called Grandma Ollie.

"Whatcha find?"

"Nothing."

"Did you look good?"

"Pretty good. I'm here in the master bedroom now. But I'm beginning to feel funny about it—"

"Why? Derek started it."

"Well the cable guy saw me. . . ." Terri told Grandma Ollie what the young man said.

"Girl, g'on and finish what you started."

"All right."

"Now, put the cable man on the phone."

"Aww come on, Grandma Ollie."

"Hurry up, this is long distance."

Terri sulked as she walked toward the den. She stuck her head in the room, "Telephone."

"It's for me?"

Terri nodded yes.

She stood there and watched as the cable man picked up the desk phone and said hello. He listened. After a few minutes, he turned purple then began stuttering.

"But I—I . . ."

The cable man began to sweat drops thicker than morning dew. He wiped his brow with the back of his hand.

"Yes, ma'am. I will. Bye."

The cable man hung up the phone. His chin dropped and a sheepish grin crossed his face. "She said for me to help you look."

And it was in the black Hefty bag of garbage that the cable man carried back in off the rear stoop that Terri found Derek's credit card statement from last month. She saw two tickets to Cancún on the billing statement and accommodations at a "couples only" spa.

By this time the cable man had finished his job and was ready to go. "What are you going to do now?" he asked.

Terri's eyes narrowed. She licked her lips as if tasting revenge. "I'm going to take back everything I gave him—the DVD player, the cashmere sweaters, all the jazz CDs. Then I'm going to the bank to close out the account we opened to pay for our wedding stuff. Then I'm going to pick him up from the airport day after tomorrow and lay his behind out."

"Cool." The cable man looked relieved. "I was worried about dog for a minute. I thought you were gonna get your grandma on him."

Terri laughed. It calmed her down, gave her direction, released tension that was gurgling inside her.

She headed to the bank where they had opened an account together several weeks before. They'd put in five thousand dollars each. The money would be used to put down payments on a reception hall and a caterer.

Terri feared that the money could be gone. Did Derek spend their money on that hoochie vacation? His and hers too? *Please not!* Not Terri's hard-earned getting-up-at-five-in-the-morning, riding-the-train, putting-in-fourteen-hours-a-day, dealing-with-drama—that money?

Heaven help Derek if he had.

Terri walked into the small black bank where they had opened this new account. The line of people, mostly elderly, made two L-shaped turns and nearly reached the front door.

Terri grunted, disgusted. Can't I catch a break? Out of

the corner of her eye, she spotted a bank specialist sitting at her desk.

She was a short woman with large black eyes: her Donna Karan suit fit well. Her auburn hair was styled with micro braids, long but neatly pinned away from her full face. Terri remembered her. She had been very helpful when she and Derek opened up the account.

Terri walked over to her and said, "Excuse me."

"Can I help you?"

"I hope so. Do you remember me? I was in a couple of months ago?"

She squinted, thought, tapping her silver Cross pen against the computer keyboard, drawing a blank.

"I'm Terri Mills. My fiancé, Derek Houser, and I opened up an account to pay for our wedding arrangements."

"Oh sure." The bank specialist smiled. "Sure. Now I remember."

Terri looked at her nameplate. "Winnie, can you help me out now? I can't stand in this long line."

"Sure," Winnie said, pointing to the chair. "Are you okay? You don't look so good."

"I just need to close out the account," Terri said, beginning to feel the emotional strain of all that she'd been through already today.

"I'm sorry, Miss Mills, but you opened the account together. I can't just close it out without Mr. Houser being here."

"But this is an emergency."

"I'm sorry. Those are the rules."

Terri stared at the woman in front of her. "I need to close the account because my fiancé is cheating on me."

Winnie blushed. "Oh, no."

"Listen, I'm not trying to get you in trouble. I'm trying to get myself out of trouble. Haven't you ever been caught up in a relationship with a man and just had your world turned up-side down?"

"But this is a business—"

"Can't you make an exception just this once? Please?" Terri hated the begging sound she heard in her own voice.

"All right. Sit down."

Terri gave the bank specialist the account number. She was relieved to find out that the money was all still there. She had Winnie divide the balance in half and give it to her in two cashier's checks. One check was made out to Terri; the other was made out to Derek.

"Thank you. Thank you. Thank you. This means so much."

"So are you gonna call off the wedding?"

Terri shrugged. She didn't want to talk about this mess any more than she had to. She shrugged again.

"Well, good luck, Miss Mills. I hope everything works out for the best."

"Thanks, Winnie," Terri said, and began hurrying toward the door.

The bank specialist watched her leave. Then she sat down and picked up the phone. She dialed a cell number. "Hello, Derek? It's me, baby. She knows!"

Chapter 4

And what Terri knew, plus what she would learn, cut her to the quick. And the quick bled memories, memories of the romantic nights she had shared with Derek.

Like in the rooftop garden last summer.

Tiny stitches of sweat cinched Terri's cotton tank top to her waist. Her dark golden thighs curled beneath her as she sat leaning over the flower bed, preparing the soil for planting.

Derek, shirtless, damp, barefooted, jeans tight in the ass, but sagging at the front waist, just below his navel, looked like a model for a Gap billboard.

He came and sat behind Terri, circled his arms around her, kissed her neck. His sturdy chest and thighs hemmed Terri in against the redwood slats of the planting bed. She drew her legs back easily then leaned her head back, letting it rest against Derek's shoulder blade. Terri wondered which was sweeter—the smell of him or the starter azaleas she was ready to plant.

Derek ran his warm, firm fingers down Terri's arms until both their hands were deep in rich, black, moist earth. You could hardly tell where their skin began and the soil ended. It was so cool against their bodies that they could barely get enough; their fingers clutched and grabbed together as they plunged deeper and deeper into the soil. It became moister, softer, and more satisfying. Then they kissed.

That summer the azaleas bloomed brighter than ever before, growing all over themselves, wild and free. A friend said admiringly, "What on earth did you use for fertilizer?"

They smiled and shrugged. Then Derek whispered in Terri's ear, "Passion."

A gentle rap at the door uprooted Terri's fond memory. She began dragging her tired legs forward, walking listlessly to the door. "Who is it?"

"It's me, Derek."

Terri snatched the door open. "You low-down dirty dog." Then she slammed the door in his face.

"Terri, let me in. Please."

"Why should I, you lying bastard!"

"Later for all the name calling. Think, Terri. Would I duck out of the conference, fly back here in the middle of the night just to lie?"

As low-down as you've been, Terri thought, I wouldn't put nothing past you. Her silence spoke mad volumes of indignation.

And Derek was feeling the sister too; loud and oh so very clear. "Behind all that being pissed off, Terri, I know you wanna hear what I have to say. You can't shut me out. Not really. I know you. You can't. So c'mon, Terri, open up."

Derek knew her stone to the bone. How'd he get so deep into my head? she wondered. Terri had to let him in now, and she did. But not untouched, not without an earful.

"You messed everything up. Couldn't keep it in your pants, had to put your jones before your engagement vows."

Derek pushed passed her. "I came to say I'm sorry."

"Sorry is for breaking a dinner date. Sorry is for breaking a vase. You. . . . broke . . . my *dapgumit* heart, boy."

Derek's gaze was direct. "There's a difference between having sex and making love. You and I make love. She and I had sex. It didn't mean anything. It was just some loose booty out there."

"Classy mouth you've got there. Goes real well with your high morals."

"Terri, you wanna be sarcastic? Be sarcastic. I'm being real with you, true with you. I was playing around before settling down. Sowing some oats. It meant nothing to me. That's the deal on that. You've got to know you're the only one who truly matters to me."

"You know what I know? I know you took Ms. Nothing to Cancún. You took her to the 'couples only' spa as a matter of fact. That whore Zelda must have gotten the thrill of her natural-born life. Until then she probably thought going on a trip was taking a bus ride to the riverboat."

"Zelda? Who's Zelda?"

Terri pulled off one of her house shoes and flung it at Derek's head—*bam!*—"You know who she is!"

Derek shrugged. Terri threw her other house shoe. *Bam!* She caught Derek on the shoulder. Terri grabbed a thick ceramic ashtray off the cocktail table.

"Hold up, girl! I know Zelda, barely. What does she have to do with us? I didn't take her to Cancún."

Terri put down the ashtray. "Will you quit it? Just quit it."

"Listen to me. I didn't cheat on you with Zelda. She doesn't have a thing to do with this. It was . . . Winnie. I met her when we opened up our bank account."

Terri's chest nerves tightened and an angry heat billowed beneath her rib cage. "You're lying."

"Think, Terri. How did I know that you were hip to my affair? Winnie called and told me that you were in the bank today. How else would I know that? She told me that you knew. I caught the next plane smoking and came right home."

Terri's legs began to tremble beneath her housecoat. It wasn't Zelda? All the times they had flirted in front of her? And it wasn't Zelda? It was that coldhearted change maker in the bank?

Terri kept her eyes steady on Derek and managed to find the couch with her hand. She felt a rush of humiliation deep in her gut as she remembered how she had begged Winnie to help her in the bank. Terri sat down stiffly against the cushions.

"After Winnie called me from the bank, I knew I had to do what I could to save our relationship." Derek sat down next to Terri.

Terri inched back as far as she could.

"Baby, that's why I broke it off with her not more than an hour ago. Then I came straight here. I'm coming clean."

Now Terri thought about how she had jammed up Zelda at her job. She moaned, "Oh God, I feel terrible."

"I can make you feel good again," Derek said, rubbing her thigh. "Let me make you feel good again."

Terri didn't even look at him. "Get away from me. You are so foul, so out of order. I don't want nothing from you."

"Maybe not tonight, because you're angry. But think. In your heart, Terri, you know that neither Zelda nor Winnie could ever hold a candle to you. I could never give them the love and the things that I still want to give and share with you."

"Get away!"

Derek pulled Terri up by the shoulders. "When you let me in, you could have slapped my face and said the wedding was off. But you didn't. Know why?"

"Tell me why, Derek."

"Because that diamond ring I put on your finger made your hand too heavy. You love me and what we are as a couple. You love it when we walk into a room and heads turn. You love the half-a-million-dollar house we've been looking at buying. You love what our children will be. You love all the things that make us *us*, and you don't want to throw it away because I made a mistake . . ."

"You screwed up."

"Every time something gets screwed up you don't toss it. Some things you fix, Terri. This is a fixer: a keeper, baby. Don't throw it away. If you do, it's on you."

"On me?" Terri growled. *The least you could do is be man enough to take the blame.*

"Baby I said I'm sorry. I did wrong but let's fix—"

"Just get away, Derek. Get away, get away, get away, Lord, get away."

"I'll go, but I won't go far. And for sure, I'll be back."

Then Derek got up and left.

Terri closed the door, and an enraged sigh, vicious and rumbling, leapt from her throat. She was no longer secure in what lay ahead for her in the area of romance. The relationship she had worked so hard to build with Derek was now broken. Terri's spirit ached as she pondered whether or not they would be able to fix it.

Chapter 5

Mending fences of the heart requires the right tools and not just the appropriate amount of desire.

Terri and Derek faced the challenge of picking up the pieces. And like with anything busted, the pieces were scattered and puzzling. They came in various shapes and sizes but with effort, patience, and care could be put back together again.

Day one: They grappled with a big piece. It lay in the center of their mess, gangly and awkward, glaringly out of order. That piece represented the ease with which they communicated and kept company with each other.

They hungered to talk, but each was leery. Derek phoned Terri first, but at a time when he knew she would be in a meeting. He was trying to feel her out.

Terri phoned back, but only after she knew that he would

be gone for the day. That night she took her receiver off the hook and cut off her cell phone too.

Day two: Derek realized that Terri wasn't helping with the big piece, so he tried to put a little one back in place instead. He sent Terri flowers, which she loved, pampering her like every good woman deserves. Terri accepted the flowers at her office, but found no joy in them. Instead she felt that the flowers were a temporary Band-Aid too small for the wound that disabled her body. She picked up the vase twice before leaving for home and put it back down each time. Terri left the flowers in her office, and not even by a window so they could drink up some sunlight. She didn't want them to live. Terri did call to say thank you, 'cause Grandma Ollie had raised her right, but she wouldn't let Derek start a conversation about their troubles. "I'm not ready to talk yet. I thought I could, but I can't. I need to think."

Day Three: Terri felt guilty because she just couldn't find the will to make up with Derek. She was so disappointed at his betrayal that it sapped all her energy. Terri sat on the side of her bed that morning, listening to the first two seconds of the four messages she had from Derek.

"Please, baby . . ."

"C'mon, baby . . ."

"Listen, girl . . ."

"Dammit, Terri . . ."

She played chopsticks with the delete button on her answering machine before falling back, emotionally tanked.

What is so hard? Terri questioned. I'm a successful black woman who doesn't mind sharing, who'll make love to a brother then make him breakfast in the morning. And what do I get? A loose zipper. A sponge that takes more respect than he gives—because he's raiding panties like a hungry kid raids the fridge.

Terri took stock of the romantic history she had with the men she'd dated. What? What is the deal? she wondered wistfully. Is there a sign on my back: "Educated Black Woman—Doesn't Need Love"? How often have I dated men who constantly throw in my face, "Oh you're so independent"?

Like it's a crime. Like I stole something out of the store. Like I did something nasty on a public street and got caught on videotape. I scuffled to get my education . . . to earn a scholarship . . . to put in dozens of hours doing work-study . . . felt the pressure to do well because my grandparents were helping all they could with their last dollars.

Wasn't I sitting in class next to you? Weren't we lab partners? Didn't we toss our caps in the air together at graduation?

What did you think I went to college for if not to get a good job and build a career? Some of my white girlfriends said their parents told them college was the place to find a husband.

That's just not what black girls are taught.

We're there looking for a way to land a good job. We have to support ourselves from the letters *G-O*. There are no trust funds or slush funds waiting till *we find that supportive husband, or ourselves.*

So we achieve. And when we do achieve, we're punished for it. We're perceived as intimidating, when all *we* want is what everyone else desires—someone to love us, to have a family with, to enjoy life. And my brothers, my brothers, it doesn't seem to matter if the date is a bus driver or an engineer, *a black woman's togetherness* causes *our separateness.*

Mr. Bus Driver: Yes, I can afford my own flowers. And theater tickets too. But would you take me? A man should romance a woman. I'd love that.

Mr. Engineer: Yes, I want a career too. Mine doesn't have to overshadow yours. Let me ride with you and not trail along behind you.

And Mr. Derek: We were so close. I thought you had broken the mold. You shared romance with me. You shared a dream of success with me. But you *shared your stuff* with somebody else.

And at some point, and this is looking and feeling like that exact point, a sister will just break down. This is definitely SMUT: Some Messed Up Trouble.

Terri sat up. It was time to swap her romance drama for her office drama. She went into the kitchen to make coffee and dropped her cup.

Terri stared down at it. Her relationship with Derek was just like the broken coffee cup, and she couldn't handle it. How, Terri thought, how in the world is this going to turn out?

Chapter 6

The how of things to come was being set in motion hundreds of miles away in places of the heart. There Grandma Ollie lay restless and she knew why. She sensed Terri was up north, hurting, tangling with a tough situation.

But Grandma Ollie resisted the urge to call her granddaughter at this time of the morning. The child needed rest. Terri needed to think. Every day she was fooling around with this dire situation involving Derek.

Grandma Ollie swung her swelled, aching legs over the side of the bed and slid down. She shuffled around in the darkness, abandoning her cane. Grandma Ollie liked to walk in the dark; it was good for her eyes to adjust to the absence of help. Kept them strong in these waning years.

Grandma Ollie walked with a sway and prayed for Terri at the same time. *You make one step, and God will make two.* That was the old saying. So each step Grandma Ollie took she said a verse . . .

"The Lord is my shepherd . . ."

Step . . . Step . . .

"I shall not want . . ."

Step . . . Step . . .

Finally she reached the kitchen and spotted a dishrag on the floor. "Oh, somebody's coming to visit!" she said to herself, reading the sign.

She picked up the dishrag and placed it on the counter. Then Grandma Ollie reached to open a cabinet and a pain caught her in the supple flesh beneath her arm. Suddenly her legs gave out and she fell. When Grandma Ollie hit the floor, she began to lose consciousness.

Falling . . . falling.

The spirit milks the mind of memories, squeezes them out in clear, pure streams, and splashes them against the circular steel container known as our past.

Grandma Ollie's unconscious thoughts were of her youth, of a freshman heart aching to choose the right man, of high hopes for love, just like Terri's.

But this memory was before Terri was even thought of, her mother too, who was Grandma Ollie's only daughter. *Before that.*

However, it was after her first real kiss in the barn, among the hay, next to the stall with the calf learning to walk on newborn legs, a kiss that left her legs just as wobbly. It was even after everyone said Ollie's older sister, Lula, had passed away. *Even after.*

Ollie was sixteen, shapely and red-boned. She hated the term because it always put to mind the cracked, suckled chicken bones left on a man's plate, a plate left for Ollie or some other female to pick up.

A whole mess of the plates were scattered on the church picnic tables. All the menfolk, and wanna-be menfolk, were huddled beneath a shady tree watching the hard-edged horseshoes beat down the soft-centered clay, trying to land a ringer.

It was a rare, cool afternoon in Collingswood, Arkansas, in late spring of 1939.

"I'm not cleaning up nary a plate," Ollie said, having watched the men and boys bonding. "I'm gonna pitch me some horseshoes."

"Ollie *thinks* she's something," she heard the other young women signify.

Ollie didn't give a care. She walked toward the ring, watching the round-bellied, bowlegged, high-behinded, and flat-footed play their game.

She pushed her way through the belts and suspenders; their universe, which was centered in the tangled steel and clay, experienced a total eclipse—an eclipse dark and round and swaying on the end of Ollie's tailbone.

She bent to pick up a pair of horseshoes and heard someone grunt, "Oomph, have mercy."

And Ollie smiled to herself, not trying to be fast really, just liking the notion of being admired and being independent all at the same time.

"Whatcha gonna do with those horseshoes, Ollie," one of the men in the group asked, "wear 'em?"

Ollie let the menfolk laugh. The foolish thought embarrassment had slipped its hand over her mouth. Really, Ollie's wit was waiting for the right moment to strike.

"True, my feet are big," she said, lifting her leg just so, swiveling her foot at the ankle. "And I love shoes."

They were mesmerized.

"But these horseshoes," she daintily clicked them together, then kicked up her heel, taking measure of one against her foot, "are too hard. I like soft-bottom shoes. I like to feel the ground I'm walking on so I can be sure of where I'm going."

"Well, well."

Ollie liked the satisfied voice of Hank. He had arrived on the end of a tailwind that kicked up over the river and broke down part of the bridge. This stranger to town had worked as hard as anyone else to fix it, and when the colored men asked, "Why?" Hank had answered, "If you want to go somewhere, sometimes you have to make a way."

What an impression he made on both colored and white folks.

"Can I play or not?" Ollie asked, looking *die-rectly* at Hank.

He stuffed his nutmeg-colored palms into the back pockets of his overalls. "All right by me."

"Lookah here," one of the older men said, "I don't see no other girl asking to play."

"They're waitin' to see what y'all gonna do about me."

"So you the volunteer."

"No, I'm the leader."

Hank chuckled. "Ollie, they don't want you to play. We can go somewhere else and *you can have a toss* with me."

"That boy's a gambling man for sure," one of the young boys howled. "Won last night and still pressin' his luck."

Ollie panicked. She'd sold a load of goods and now had to deliver. Her heart lurched. This was a real man; not one of the boys she went to school with, the ones she could out-think on any given day that the good Lord made.

These broad shoulders of Hank's had carried a sack of clothes across the South, going here and there, fending for his twenty-one-year-old self. Baby-fine hair rusted auburn by the sun was slicked down on his crown with peach juice. Neck muscles. Arm muscles. All rippled from hard work. He had a mannish air. He had a sweet presence. Hank looked like Christmas unwrapped.

"Comin'?" Hank asked, the word hanging off his lips like a lure on a hook. "Comin'?"

Too proud not to take the bait, Ollie simply followed when Hank started walking away toward Lovers Rock, a small cliff that overlooked the river. Hank knew the way well.

What happened next at Lovers Rock would change her life forever. Grandma Ollie would have to tell Terri all about it . . . and about other times in her life too; some stories fresh, other stories reminders . . . because, as she now knew from the sign, it was Terri who would be coming to visit.

Chapter 7

"Is it time for your visit?" Dr. Candi asked, slipping the stethoscope from around her neck so she could embrace her old college buddy. "I thought your checkup was scheduled for next month."

"I'm late."

Dr. Candi felt Terri tense so she hugged her a little bit longer. "How late?"

"Three days."

"Awww, girl. That's not long. Stress can throw you off, a change in diet, any old thing."

"I need to know."

"Why didn't you just get a kit?" Dr. Candi laughed, "Anyway, it's not like you don't love the daddy. You're getting mar—"

Terri's cold stare told the story.

"I'm not in the mood for drugstore prophecies. I want hard-core science. Can you get the lab results back today?"

"For my sorority sister? Not a problem. I've got your back."

That brought a warm smile from Terri.

Dr. Candi sat next to Terri on the examination table. She tapped her left shoulder. "You wanna put your head right there and have a good cry?"

"Not unless you want a snot shampoo."

They both laughed.

Several minutes later, Dr. Candi walked Terri to the elevator. "I'll have the results by one. Call your office?"

"Wouldn't dare be anywhere else; I've got a real big case."

"Your job is a stress monster. C'mon, Tee. I'm a gynie not a psychiatrist. Take it easy."

"I'll try."

And that's just what Terri's secretary had been doing back at the office, trying and trying to reach her.

"I paged you a gazillion times. I even left a message on your answering machine at home."

Terri loved her secretary, Haji; she loved her Jamaican accent, her braids, her sturdy work ethic, her *I'm leading the parade* walk, and her flair for the dramatic.

"Sorry, my pager's shot. What happened? The office was on fire?" Terri teased. Everything was urgent to Haji.

"I got an emergency call—"

"And?"

"Maybe you should sit down."

"Haji, please. Out with it already."

Terri's secretary took a deep breath and exhaled.

"The preview terms for the out-of-court settlement didn't get to Baxter and Associates."

Terri felt a bomb go off in her head. "How'd that happen?"

Haji reached up and twisted one of her braids. Her voice steadied. "The courier service had a problem."

"A problem? As much money as we spend with them? It better be a major disaster or we're dropping our account."

"Terri, you know how it is now. They had a suspicious package, so they cleared out the whole building. The police came and checked; turned out to be nothing, but by then the whole office was messed up. Our package got lost."

"Well, let me call up Baxter and tap dance, then we'll just shoot over another copy."

Haji reached up and began twisting another braid.

"What-what?" Terri dropped her chin and gazed up at Haji. "Now what?"

"Remember? I was out with the flu the day the document was pulled together. We had a temp. Apparently she didn't save a copy on disk."

Terri sat down and sighed. "Haji, you ever feel like the world is a black cocktail dress and you're a pair of brown pumps?"

Haji giggled and relaxed. She grabbed a cup and headed across the room for some coffee. "Sounds like one of Grandma Ollie's old sayings."

"Hmmmm-huh." Terri closed her eyes and moaned. "I need to call her too." She opened her eyes. "But first grab the file with all my notes. I've gotta pull this bad boy together again and make sure it gets to Baxter by five."

"They're already there. The red folder at your right elbow."

Terri smiled. Haji was great at taking the initiative. "Hold all calls—except Dr. Candi."

Haji lifted her cup of coffee in a "will do" salute and put a hurry on.

Terri's mind was like the cards of a Rolodex; flipping from one thought to another. Suppose she was pregnant? What then? What would Grandma Ollie say?

How funky would Baxter & Associates be about this late delivery of terms? They could get very salty, might even try to change a term or two to make the city eat a little crow. Suppose the legal director found out? Morgan? Sometimes he was cool as a cucumber—other times he was hot as a chili pepper. The mistake wasn't Terri's fault, but she was determined to fix it. And fix it fast.

Terri slaved for nearly two hours before her line rang; ten seconds later Haji burst into the room.

"Dr. Candi?"

"No." Haji shook her head. "Security. Someone vandalized your car."

Terri ran downstairs to find that the tires on her Beemer had been sliced and diced. All she could do was step back and throw up her hands.

"I went to grab some coffee," the elderly guard began to explain.

Terri leaned back on the car, holding down her anger, barely able to absorb the explanation.

"Got this medicine to take, Ms. Mills." The guard held up a prescription bottle.

What did Grandma Ollie always tell her?

When you're mad, don't act; wait until you calm down. A mad mind makes reckless mistakes.

"Wasn't gone two seconds hardly."

Terri's head began to ache.

"But don't you worry, the security camera's got 'em. We double-record; that was my idea. Come see, Ms. Mills."

They walked over to the security hut. There was barely enough room for the two of them to stand inside. The guard reached up, stopped one tape, and rewound it. He flicked a switch on the monitor and what Terri saw gripped her insides.

"Gotcha," the guard said triumphantly. "See her?"

Sure I do, Terri thought. I know that face, that walk. Although the sexy sway was now a hurried sneak. Sure I do.

Zelda.

Terri leaned in, squinting. After the last tire was slashed, Zelda slipped a piece of paper inside the door handle on the passenger side.

Terri rushed over to the car. What was it? She rounded the trunk, grabbed the note. It read, "Lawyers know other lawyers. Secretaries know other secretaries. You blew my chance. I blew your tires. Z."

And the *Z* was cut like Zorro.

"Doggone drama queen," Terri cursed under her breath.

What did Grandma Ollie always say?

What goes around comes around; and when it's some wrongdoing, it comes around quicker.

Damn, Terri thought, this came back to me quicker than the speed of light.

"The police will be here any minute, Ms. Mills."

"Forget about it; just let it go. I'll call my mechanic. He'll tow the car, slap some tires on it, and have it back to me by the end of the day."

"But I already called—"

Terri gave the guard a firm look. "Let it go."

"Yes, ma'am."

Terri thought to herself in the elevator, What else can go wrong? Can the disaster gods focus on someone else for a change?

The disaster gods have tunnel vision.

The elevator doors opened and who was standing there? None other than Terri's boss, Morgan.

"Terri, I was just heading to your office."

"Hi, Morgan. My car was in an accident in the garage." A worried thought exploded inside Terri's brain: Does he know about Baxter & Associates?

"Nothing serious, I hope."

"No, not at all, Morgan. What's up?"

Morgan began walking and Terri fell right in step. "I got a call from Baxter and Associates. You know, whenever we go up against those guys we nail 'em. But something's up this time. All of a sudden they've decided not to settle."

Again Grandma Ollie's words came to mind? *Sometimes the game gets the hunter.*

He knows about the brief that never got there, Terri reasoned; better lay it on the line. "There was a mix-up with our courier service; settlement terms didn't reach them by the deadline. I decided to handle it myself, Morgan.

B and A had agreed over the phone to accept it today by five."

"Now they're flip-flopping again."

"I guess they think they can turn our oversight into their opportunity."

"And if I know you, Terri, you'll make 'em regret it, right?"

"Absolutely."

"Good."

Morgan headed to his office and Terri went to hers; Haji was standing at the door waiting.

"Dr. Candi called."

Terri tried to read Haji's face. She knew her sorority sister knew better than to tell her secretary the deal, but Haji picked up on stuff like a magnet. Did she sense Terri's dilemma?

"She left a message, insisted on voice mail." Haji looked insulted.

Terri tried to act nonchalant. But her heart pounded, Run to the desk, run to the desk.

Haji, with her nosy behind, just stood there. "She sounded urgent, Terri."

Terri shrugged and walked over to her desk—slowly, but man was it killing her. Would you go already? Terri glanced at Haji. Would you? Terri sat at her desk and shrugged at Haji. "Thank you."

Haji's face fell faster than the house that landed on the wicked witch of the west.

Terry yanked up the receiver as soon as her door slammed. She hit the play button. Am I? She wondered. Am I? Terri anxiously awaited Dr. Candi's voice, but instead she got an earful of a classic tune.

"Happy days are here again . . ."

Then Dr. Candi said, "I usually play that for the couples who want to get pregnant. But I thought it worked for you too *since you're not!*"

Terri spun around in her chair and clicked her heels together. "Candi, you're a trip."

"So cheer up, Terri, you're in the clear. Oh yeah, how's Grandma Ollie? Give her my love. Bye."

Terri hit the disconnect button then quickly dialed Grandma Ollie's phone number.

Grandma Ollie was the first to show Terri God, and because of that she'd been able to enjoy him ever since.

So it was God's name Terri called when her cousin answered the phone and told her Grandma Ollie was sick and in the hospital.

It was God's book of Psalms that Terri read so that her spirit would remember that she should fear no evil.

It was God's guidance that told Terri to ask her boss for time off to go see about Grandma Ollie.

Terri knew she was in the middle of a killer case too; it was a backbreaker, a soul-shaker, and a career-maker. But God's guidance said, Ask and you shall be given, seek and you shall find.

Terri had no idea that by asking she would be given an opportunity to find her way through a professional crossroads.

"Morgan," she said, sitting in the oak, leather-bound chair in her boss's office. "I need time to be with my grandmother. She's ill."

What was it about Morgan that had lured Terri to work for him?

His face. That's what Terri remembered now as she waited for Morgan's reply. His face looked powerful: square chin, steady dark eyes, head full of gray hair, high cheekbones, always a hint of tan from his weekend golf outings.

It was a powerful face. It was an honest face. That's why when Morgan *came out of his face* Terri was completely surprised.

"Terri," he asked, "have I always treated you fairly?"

"Yes."

"May I speak freely then?"

"By all means."

Morgan leaned back in the chair, *and then came out of his face.*

"Often I hear black women complain about not being given the same opportunities as white men. They say they're held back, not allowed to reach their potential. I assigned you one of the most important cases to hit the city in a decade. Do you think a white man would come in here and ask to leave a case like that because his grandmother slipped in the kitchen?"

It was as if the universe suddenly began playing a kid's game: "One, two, three . . . Red light!" Everything froze: Terri's face, her throat, and her eyes, even her brain.

"Don't answer right away. Think about it and come back at the end of the day and we'll talk."

For the rest of the day Terri thought and she burned.

What was Morgan really asking her? What was the motive behind the question?

He was asking Terri to be a player in his game, to keep her eye focused on the ball; he wanted her to smack it, run the bases with abandon, and slide headfirst into home. Never mind if the bat broke and sailed into the stands and hit a fan.

Never mind that.

Morgan wanted to know if Terri could be professional without being personal.

Terri swiveled her black power chair back and forth. She wanted to thrive in the world of the big boys. She'd worked hard for it. Her ambition lived in the world of the big boys, but her heart lived in a village. That's what her answer to Morgan would be.

"Morgan, have I always worked hard for you?"

"Yes," he answered, leaning back in his chair.

"Then may I speak freely?"

"Yes."

"Morgan, when black people were brought to America as slaves, they lost their language, their way of life, but managed to hang on to some customs, like the African proverb 'It takes a village to raise a child.' "

"Hillary Clinton's book."

"She borrowed the proverb, but black folks live it."

"You lost me, Terri."

"Everyone pitches in, Morgan. My Grandma Ollie stepped in to fill a role in my life, she raised me. She's the only mother I've ever known. It takes a village."

"Who's with her now?"

"My cousins."

"Well, there's your village. Why don't you work during the week and fly to see your grandmother on the weekends?"

"But Grandma Ollie wasn't a weekend mother to me. She's been a mother day in and day out. I need a short leave— say six weeks?"

"I thought you were a player."

"You know I am."

"I thought you were going places."

"I will."

What was that Grandma Ollie had always told her?

Baby, when you know you right, stick to your guns. Sometimes confidence can win a compromise.

"Terri," Morgan sighed. "I'll tell you what I'll do. This case with Baxter and Associates is going to take some fleshing out. Your associates can handle that with some conference-call supervision from you. Take the six weeks, that's it. I can hold off till then, but if you're not back, Terri—"

"I'll be back."

Morgan appeared disappointed. "You know you're admired for being a tough lawyer, a go-to lawyer, and when you come back some of that reputation will have crumbled."

"I'll catch what crumbles," Terri promised, "and build it back up into solid rock."

Chapter 8

Souls say there's magic on Lovers Rock. That there, a country boy's peck has the power of Prince Charming's kiss; that a country duckling becomes a swan in the eye of the beholder.

Terri's plane swooned over the heart-shaped stone as it headed in for a landing at the tiny airport in Collingswood, Arkansas. At one time Terri thought she and Derek had magic. He'd left two messages on her answering machine at home; she'd erased them as soon as she heard his voice. Could Terri forgive Derek? Could she ever trust him again? Terri didn't know.

But what she did know was that Grandma Ollie looked old. This thought struck Terri as she stood in the doorway of the hospital room and gazed at her. Was it her hair, parted down the middle and rolled up into those two tiny balls?

Was it the pasty color of Grandma Ollie's skin, always cream, but today a soupy gray?

Was it the paper-thin hospital gown? It was bleached white although the original gold color could still be seen in the stringed bow tied at the front of her neck.

Grandma Ollie opened her eyes. "Well, look what the wind done blew in."

"A wind called Delta Airlines."

Terri dropped her bags and hugged Grandma Ollie. She smelled like baby oil and pet milk. "You look good, girl."

"Don't you stand there and tell that tale," Grandma Ollie fussed, scooting up in the bed. "These folks got me looking worse than Granny from *The Beverly Hillbillies*."

"They do not."

"Pah-shaw! You know I have more style and flair than this. Couldn't catch up with that trifling cousin of yours to bring me my good gowns. My cologne. My good twenty-five-dollar house slippers. I was gonna give them some fashion in here."

"What did the doctor say?"

"Look at my hair. I didn't wear plaits when I was a chile. They have medical students coming in here poking around. Can't tell young folks ah thing. Nothing at all."

"Has the doctor made his rounds today?"

"That Dr. Welby wanna-be? That man looks like he needs medication more than me. He's bent over and slow. I tell you, that's the funniest walking joker I've ever laid eyes on."

"Give him a break, Grandma Ollie."

"He walks like a pigeon that's been fed a pan of biscuits. And the man wants to operate on my hip."

"Surgery? When?"

Grandma Ollie rolled her eyes. "You too young to be

going deaf. I didn't say I was gonna let them cut on me. No ma'am. They like to experiment on old folks in these hospitals nowadays."

"Grandma Ollie, if the doctor says you need surgery, you need it."

"They'll say that just to let those students get some practice in. You think the old doctor is the one doing the operating, but instead it's one of those youngsters running around here with a pocketknife."

"Stop tripping, Grandma Ollie. I don't think they'd let the students train on you. And I don't think the doctor would suggest surgery if you didn't need it."

"Listen here, girl: Did you come here to be a help or a caution?"

Terri sighed; she can't be that sick, she's still feisty as hell. Terri lifted the white sheet and saw the purple and crimson hip, swelled. "Does it hurt?"

"Only when people talk about cutting on it."

A knuckle rap against the door drew their attention. A group of medical students stood in the doorway. They were six in number. Eager-looking. Alert-looking. Young-looking.

Grandma Ollie cupped her hand against her mouth and whispered to Terri. "That's them. The doctors of *Dawson's Creek*."

"May we come in?" one of the med students asked.

Grandma Ollie went into her sweet role. "Well, as you children know, my door always swings on welcome hinges—but today my granddaughter, Terri, is here visiting. We'd like some time to ourselves."

The group murmured.

"You can come back later." Grandma Ollie put some strap in her voice. "Run on now. *Run on.*"

And they left.

How does she do that? Terri wondered. How does Grandma Ollie get people to do what she wants all the time? Sometimes she's sweet. Sometimes she's sassy. Sometimes she's mean. But all the time, to Terri, she seemed to get her way. Grandma Ollie stays in control. How does she do it?

"Grandma Ollie, you're here to get better. Not to run the hospital."

"Enough on that. What happened 'tween you and Derek?"

"You want me to be sick too?" Terri joked, but for real, the mention of Derek's name caused a queasy feeling in her gut.

But compassion filled Grandma Ollie's eyes. And Terri found courage in those eyes . . . the same eyes that had told her that scraped knees would heal . . . those same eyes were wells now, willing to hold Terri's pain. And when she'd emptied out her story, Grandma Ollie threw her arms open. Terri flew into them. For the first time in a long time she felt truly comforted.

"Did I ever tell you about my first beau, Hank? And Lovers Rock?"

"No, ma'am."

"I was sixteen and didn't rightly know what to do with myself. I felt cocky but on edge, unsure, both of those things at the same time. See here, my body and my mind was both changing in leaps and bounds . . ."

That was part of the reason that Ollie followed Hank that

day, up to Lovers Rock. She had to go, had to know what mystery lay there. Oh, she'd been to Lovers Rock before with a couple of silly boys, but they'd only grinned and ducked their heads. She'd felt nothing, but understood in her heart that this place was special. But *special* is not a word to throw around loose like change; when you say it you should mean it. When you feel it you should say it.

Ollie felt something special about Hank and she wanted to know more; her mind was inquisitive. What's this love thang the old folks warn you about? This love thang that's so powerful that women stagger down dirt roads at night crying their eyes out? That men get their switchblades and threaten to cut a friend every which way but loose?

Lovers Rock was glorious; the heart-shaped stone still glistened from the rain that morning. In the brush surrounding it were shady trees, glittering green, and little sprouting flowers managed to shimmy themselves out from in between the pebbles.

"Sho is pretty up here," Ollie said.

"Prettier now that you're here," Hank replied.

And he said it like a common truth—like . . . the sun's up or it's planting season—which made Ollie wonder how come no one else had ever told her how pretty she was before.

Hank came and stood beside Ollie and placed his hands around her waist, and leaned her back for a kiss.

"Wait now," Ollie blurted out, pushing him away.

"Don't be afraid, Ollie. I won't hurt you."

Ollie relaxed but her mind warned, Move away, girl.

"Aww," Hank uttered almost as an aside, "Ollie, girl.

Every time I see you, I smile. Every time you see me, you smile."

Distance gave Ollie courage.

"Maybe I smile because you always carrying those honey jugs you paid to deliver. I love honey."

"I love sweet things too," Hank whispered, plowing the distance between them in half.

"I don't think I should be here," Ollie whispered back.

"We should be here just like the trees over there. Just like the flowers. We belong here, Ollie. This is Lovers Rock. Naturally we belong."

What's going on here? Ollie wondered. Why do I feel like I want to run but I have to stay? Is it the magic they say is up here? Is that what I'm feeling?

Ollie's heart was thumping, the way a bird pecks at the ground, quickly and methodically. She felt flush and warm, like a roasting fire simmered in her belly. She was uncomfortable but doggone it if she didn't like it.

"It's natural, Ollie," Hank explained, putting that last bit of distance between them out to pasture. "All natural, look around, and see."

Hank slipped his arms around her waist.

"Wait now . . . ," Ollie whispered. He feels so warm and safe. But still home training made her say, "Wait now . . ."

"We gonna wait, Ollie, and watch . . ."

He smells like honey, Ollie thought, and sturdy sweet, pure, just like that honey he lugs around in those jars.

"Watch here, any minute the wind is gonna rise up, and watch that branch there, that pretty little branch just above our heads. You're the branch and I'm the wind. Watch, Ollie, watch now."

And when the wind came it was forceful but gentle, confident and steady. The wind eased down the inside of the branch; the little leaves on the tip shivered gently. The wind's strength grew, and individual limbs extending from the branch twisted slowly left, then slowly right, making a soft whipping sound.

The wind continued to push, building to a gust. The little leaves on the branch's tip stood straight up while the limb itself dipped down then snapped back up against the air only to . . . hang there . . . hang there till the gust died down first to a breeze then to a whisper.

"Terri, that's how I truly learned about the natural order of things," Grandma Ollie said, "through sight and showing up on Lovers Rock with Hank. Hank, the first to make me feel real love."

Terri lifted her head from Grandma Ollie's shoulder. "And you two were in love a long time?"

A faraway look filled Grandma Ollie's eyes. "A long time, until . . ."

"Until what, Grandma Ollie?"

She smiled down at Terri. "Until the fire in the barn."

"May I come in?"

A doctor knocked at the door—wrinkled white coat, green scrubs, five pens in his right pocket, shiny bald head with a brown spot that resembled a burned-out bulb, square block glasses, silver frames, a slow, slow walk as he moved forward.

"Yeah, you can come in if you're planning on letting me out," Grandma Ollie bartered. "Please do."

Terri knew her grandmother. She was thinking, My grand-baby is here now; I'm gonna show out and get out of this hospital right now.

"Hello, Doctor. I'm Terri Mills, Miss Ollie's granddaughter."

"All the way from Chicago on Delta Airlines," Grandma Ollie bragged, "first class."

"No coach?" The doctor grinned.

"Only her bags!" Grandma Ollie hurrahed.

Terri cut her eyes toward the hospital bed.

Grandma Ollie rolled her eyes back and tucked the covers around her legs in a very dainty fashion.

The doctor pulled out a tiny flashlight and began looking at Grandma Ollie's eyes. "Everything okay? Anything unusual today?"

"The food was hot."

"Okay, Miss Ollie." The doctor chuckled as he pulled out a wooden tongue depressor. "Open wide."

"Put a Popsicle on that stick and I'll think about it."

"Grandma Ollie, be serious," Terri scolded. "Doc, are you going to have to operate on my grandmother's hip?"

"Well—"

"Speaking for myself, I don't want to be cut on like some Parker House sausage on a breakfast plate. Don't believe we'll be having any surgery."

The doctor winked. "Visiting hours are just about over. Terri, can we talk in the hallway?"

"Y'all can talk about it. Write a newspaper article about it. Whatsomevers. I'm not in the mood for cutting."

Terri and the doctor moved outside into the hallway.

"Oh, that's low-down. Y'all know I can't hear you way out there. Talk up."

The doctor whispered, "I think we should do the surgery. Three years ago we went in and put a metal plate in that hip. Well, when your grandmother fell, the plate shifted some and that's why she's not healing quickly enough. If we don't go in now, and wait, she could have a problem with the plate and pain."

Grandma Ollie yelled a hoarse request, sounding like the cartoon character Foghorn Leghorn. "I say, I say y'all speak up."

"Is there any danger with the surgery itself, Doctor?"

He paused. "Every surgery is dangerous, especially at your grandmother's age. But really I don't foresee any problems. You're grandmother is a diabetic. I'd have to wait until her blood sugar settles down, but I think it will be okay."

"Terri, Terri, you come on in here right now. I mean it, c'mon now. Don't make me haftah get out of this bed."

"I'm a grown woman." Terri shrugged, playing bad for the doctor. Then her face got a little worried. "She can't get out of that bed, can she?"

The doctor laughed. "No, Miss Ollie can't. But we want her to. Soon. So your job is to convince her to have this surgery. Can you?"

Chapter 9

"No, you can't," Sugar said as she drove the Geo down the dirt road. "Girl, how you gonna get your grandma to do something she don't wanna? Them Andersons are some mean, stubborn folk. Take it from your cousin, I live down here. I know."

Lisa got the nickname Sugar because she used to suck her thumb as a child. Her grandmother and Grandma Ollie were first cousins; Grandma Ollie decided to put a halt to Lisa's thumb sucking by putting cayenne pepper on her hand.

Didn't work.

Lisa would sneak into the kitchen, roll her thumb around in the sugar jar, then suck on it all day long anyway. After she had outsmarted both old ladies, everyone started calling her Sugar.

"Mama, I want a mountain bike like Jimmy," the little boy in the backseat whined.

That was Sugar's eight-year-old son, William. He looked like Sugar. Sucked his thumb like Sugar. Was a chip off the old Sugar block—so, of course, they nicknamed him Cube.

"Hush, boy, don't you hear me talking to cousin Terri?"

Sugar wasn't one for shortcuts—she was taking the long way to Grandma Ollie's house and she hadn't cut down a bit on her intake of sweets. Sugar weighed over two hundred pounds and was only about five-five. But contrary to the big-girl stereotype, Sugar was graceful. She was a snappy dresser too and loved to flaunt her size in front of men.

"But I want a mountain bike like Jimmy. Say yeah, Ma!"

Sugar whispered to Terri, "Remember this one?" She turned around to Cube, "If Jimmy jumps in the lake, you gonna jump in the lake too?"

"No," Cube drawled, "I'm get me ah ride on that bike."

"Cube, you ah mess." Sugar promised lightheartedly, "We'll see, baby."

"Aawwww," Cube whined.

"Sugar, you might be able to use some of that money you were saving to fly in for my wedding."

"Shut yo' mouth," Sugar hissed. "What he'd do?"

Terri motioned her head toward Cube in the backseat.

"Cube ain't listening, girl."

"Am too. Listening to hear if I'm gonna get me a new bike."

Sugar rolled her eyes. "Tell me later, cuz."

The Geo grunted around the last bend as they came within a dozen yards of the Anderson family home. "There's the old place, still standing after nearly a century."

Yolanda Joe

Terri hadn't been to Collingswood in quite a while. Where
had the time gone? Terri was working and her vacations were
spent with Derek, trying to shore up that relationship. Wonder what he's doing? Terri thought. She looked at her watch.
Seven o'clock. Friday. He's at the after-work set at the South
Loop Jazz Scene. A picture of Derek grinding on some face-
less fleshy-behind girl flashed in her head.

Terri threw the thought out of her mind and began to
focus on the house. It looked ancient, especially by today's
standards, even for a small southern town, but Terri loved the
sight of it.

The heavy, thick grass was a lush green; Terri remembered
how burned-out yellow it would get in the summertime,
while still feeling as soft as hay. The house itself was built out
of thick frame slats, cut from logs that once graced the
Arkansas woods. Grandma Ollie's father had floated the wood
downriver on a barge himself. It was a fairly large house with
a great room, a dining room with a window, and three bed-
rooms, all square-shaped and on one level.

"You okay from here?" Sugar asked. "I'm late for work and
I gotta drop off Cube at his granny's."

"I'll be fine," Terri said, grabbing her bags. She found the
old set of keys in her pocket; the ones she'd had as a child, still
on the end of a twisted piece of yarn. Like all things familiar,
the key slid into the lock and opened the door as if she'd uttered magic words.

"There's that crazy lamp," Terri mumbled as she dropped
her bags just inside the door.

The lamp was porcelain, shaped like a pilgrim ship with

68

pieces of marquis-cut glass hanging from the neck. It cast a slight figure now, not nearly as impressive as it was sitting on the cocktail table years ago in their home in Chicago.

When Terri was ten, she thought the lamp had once belonged to Aladdin. She would grab the lamp and rub it, wishing for things, things she deserved but was denied . . . things like a real mother who wasn't old-fashioned and who would let her stay out after the streetlights came on; who wouldn't say no every time she wanted to go to a sleepover; who wouldn't ask fifty million questions whenever she walked out the door on Saturday to play.

Terri recalled an incident when she was thirteen and had a crush on a boy named Bobby who lived across the tracks. Grandma Ollie didn't like Bobby; said he acted too slick, his lips were too big, and he talked out of the side of his mouth.

Bobby was the coolest boy in the neighborhood; could fight the best, rap the best, and ride his bike the fastest.

Grandma Ollie called Terri into the house one day. She told Terri she'd heard through the grapevine that Terri and Bobby were going together.

What grapevine? Terri thought. There are no grapevines on the south side of Chicago. And if there were, the drunks would strip 'em bare trying to make some free wine.

Grandma Ollie stood over Terri and questioned the girl till her breath smelled from all the accusations and Terri's eyes filled with tears.

Grandma Ollie told Terri to invite Bobby over to the house, they could sit on the bench in the backyard and talk. If Terri was gonna keep company, it needed to be where Grandma Ollie could see them.

Terri sensed a setup, a trick, a grandmother drive-by; what was she going to do? Grandma Ollie could say enough crazy, old-time stuff to embarrass a mailbox. But what could Terri do? Not a thing, child, but cross her fingers and her toes and invite the boy over.

The two kids were actually having a good time, laughing and talking; Bobby even brought his radio, blasting their favorite station.

Then Grandma Ollie came out of the house. She had power, child. She stared at the radio that was playing too loud—and swear to God, the batteries died. She walked over to Terri, who was sitting on the bench wearing a short-sleeve sweater and a skirt.

"Hi, Mr. Bobby."

"Hello," he said, shaking his boom box, wondering what the heck was wrong with his radio.

Grandma hex, Terri thought; Eveready *ain't ready* for that.

Grandma Ollie pulled out a crisp five-dollar bill, held it up, and said, "Terri, can you hold this for me?"

"Sure," Terri said, reaching for the money.

Grandma Ollie intentionally dropped the bill.

Instinctively Terri caught it between her knees.

"Whenever you're around boys from now on, keep your legs closed just that tight. Don't let that five-dollar bill drop, baby. 'Cause if you start opening your legs wide enough to let it fall, you just might lose something else too."

Terri leaned back on the couch now and remembered how embarrassed she was at the time. Now Grandma Ollie's brass struck her funny.

Terri played with the bangles on her magic lamp, tired from her trip and exhausted from all the drama in her life. Suddenly an urge began growing in her heart.

Call Derek; call him.

Terri glanced down at the diamond ring on her finger. It was loose. Physically loose. But now its romantic fit was the very definition of loose—as in vague, slack, and indefinite.

Call Derek; call him.

When does the heart grow up? When a girl's legs are long enough for silk stockings? Or when her hips can fill out a dress? When she can dance in four-inch heels and it sounds like thunder clapping?

Or is it more complicated than that? Is it when she can set eyes on a handsome boy and not flush red and giggle?

When she can kiss out of possibility and not out of passion? Terri wondered if there was a place in the soul that was like a door with growth marks notched into the grain. If her romantic soul had growth marks, how high would the notches go?

Runt level, Terri thought as she used her cell phone to call Derek. It had a star-six-nine blocker on it—Terri still didn't want Derek to know where she was.

The shrill ring that began was a sad song playing in Terri's ear. What am I going to say? She wondered. Say everything I'm feeling? No, just a little bit of it.

But would that be worth it? How can you carve off a sliver of hurt and actually do the emotion justice? How slight and unimpressive that would be, like a flickering crescent compared with a full moon.

Derek's voice rattled, yet soothed Terri. She needed just a taste of it, like a smoker needs a hit off a cigarette when they're first trying to quit.

Terri wanted to kick herself, first off for calling, and secondly for letting Derek say "Hello? Hello?" without a single response.

She killed the line and closed her eyes, reaching out for the lamp. Her nails ran along the rough edges of the glass before finding the smooth body of the lamp. Terri rubbed it. She wondered, Will my wish come true?

The next morning, she awoke to the sun bursting through the window. It had been tough to fall asleep at first because there was no noise. What's up with that? she'd thought, watching the minutes tick by. Can a sister get a car horn honking? A door slamming? I mean, my God, we are still living in the world. Now that morning had arrived, Terri felt better, somewhat rested. She clasped her arms together and stretched them overhead like wings. When those wings found their way back down to her sides, Terri rolled over and grabbed the phone.

"Hi Haji, this is Terri . . . Good, flight was fine . . . Thanks; I'll tell her you asked about her. Are the associates on board with the briefs they have to file? We can't let Baxter and Associates sucker punch us again . . . Everything's good? . . . Smooth sailing, huh? That's Gladys Knight to my ears, girl. Call me if there's any problem—day or night—hit my cell. And no, you're doing right. I'm still in meetings or out with a client whenever Derek calls. I'll be in touch. Thanks."

Terri heard her cousin Sugar come in.

"Moooornin'!" Sugar mooed like a cow proud of a pail of milk.

I'm not getting up! Terri vowed, slinking down in the cozy bed. Couldn't remember the last time she was still in bed at nine in the morning.

"Mooornin', sleepyhead."

I'm not getting up!

"Oh, you ain't planning to eat then, huh? Nobody gets breakfast in bed around here, cuz, except Grandma Ollie."

Sugar's catcalling couldn't budge Terri, but the smell of bacon and eggs frying finally got her out of bed. She shuffled to the kitchen, yawning and tousling her hair with her hands.

Terri stopped by the large window in the dining area and glanced back at the clearing in the rear of the house. It had been there forever. It was a large square ground, no grass, just dirt, never seemed to have any purpose. "Say, Sugar, I always wondered, What used to be back there?"

"Some old barn. Some old barn that burned down eons ago."

Chapter 10

"So you wanna know about the barn?" Grandma Ollie said with a slight smile. "What for, baby?"

"Because it has something to do with you and Hank. You said that you two loved one another for a long time, until the barn burned down. How many barn burnings can there be in one person's life?"

"Well, let a body see . . . get comfortable . . . the story is as long as the hair on your head."

Terri scooted closer to the side of the hospital bed. "I'm listening."

"I'll speak on it for as long as I can before I wear out. That's a promise, baby. Let's see here now; I started falling in love with Hank oh way back . . ."

Ollie had begun to love Hank not because of their secret meetings up on Lovers Rock where his tongue was thick and sweet; or because his fingertips were slightly sticky too and against her skin felt as if he couldn't let her go even if he had ah mind to.

No, Ollie had begun to love Hank because of the way he showed her things. When the sky was tore up with brooding clouds and torrential rain, Hank pointed out that the drops falling on the tin roof of the church sounded like bells.

"My mama told me," Hank explained one day up on Lovers Rock, as they sat arm in arm, "that since I was born on Christmas I was touched by an angel. That's why I always see the bright side of things."

And it was that touch that made both men and women want to be around Hank. They wanted to be in his presence, to pitch horseshoes, to drink 'shine, to gamble on cards with the colored boys at the juke joint, to make love, to buy honey—reversing that, yes the ladies really loved Hank.

Ollie's father did not. "He too . . . too . . ."

"Too what, Daddy?"

"Too wild." He watched Ollie roll her eyes. "Watch out those marble eyes don't roll clean out of your head. And watch that boy every minute. I am."

Hank was an immensely prideful man. He was one line in the sand away from being arrogant. And although this is the angels' honest truth, it is a bit misleading. That's because Hank's pride was not of the bitter variety, of the wanton *what I'm holding is more than what you have* or *what I am makes me better than you* kind. Hank's pride was actually driven by intense amazement at what he could attain or accomplish through wit and hard work. Where others stumbled, Hank sprinted forward. What turned up barren in the land of others sprang up tall and green in Hank's backyard.

The primary source of Hank's pride in Collingswood was his success in the honey business. Hank gathered honey for Mr. Forester, a wealthy white landowner on the edge of town, known for being cheap. Legend had it that he once broke a man's toe with a gun butt for standing on a coin he'd dropped. Hank was among four other colored men who collected the honey, bottled and sold it for Mr. Forester. They reported daily to a white man named Paul.

All the colored folks called him Penny Less Paul behind his back because he was as poor as they. His white skin provided the one step that put him above Hank and the other colored workers. And of those colored workers, Hank was the sweetest. His set of honeycombs produced more nectar than any of the other two put together. Despite that, he and every other man, including Penny Less Paul, were underpaid. And they all knew it.

One day Mr. Forester brought a group of Atlanta businessmen to the honey farm. Hank had asked Ollie to come ahead of time and make a table display of sweets made with the honey. Ollie baked a couple of pies, cookies, and made some ice tea. Then she picked some flowers and arranged them around a stack of honey jars.

Hank admired the display. "Girl, girl, everything you touch turns to pretty."

Mr. Forester and the Atlanta businessmen rode their horses to the center of the farm, where Hank and Penny Less Paul were waiting. The two men were standing on a promise. If they made a good showing, Mr. Forester swore he'd give them both a big bonus. The businessmen climbed down from their horses and examined the stacked jars that glistened as if they were filled with liquid gold.

Mr. Forester picked up a jar in each hand. "We can start shipping you honey for your new restaurant as soon as we sign the contract. There is no finer honey this side of the Mississippi."

One of the men challenged, "I've heard about it far and wide, sure. But can you keep it coming? We expect quite a demand."

Penny Less Paul hesitated. "How much you think?"

Mr. Forester whipped him an angry look. "Doesn't matter."

Hank beamed with pride. "The more you want, the more you'll get. Guaranteed. Look . . ."

Hank took the men to his combs, touting the honey all the way. The thick, deep orange sweetness slithered out of the combs and down the sides of the trees like the snake in the Garden of Eden. It was enticing to the tongue too. Ollie and the other colored folks swore that Hank's honey tasted better than anyone else's, and even kept longer. After the businessmen sampled the sweets Ollie had prepared, the deal was sealed.

Mr. Forester whispered to Penny Less Paul, "Old Hank charmed the deal through. How you let that colored boy outshine you?"

Hank and Ollie never heard the remark. They were too busy hugging and grinning all over each other. Hank told her to pick out a new dress and a new hat. He had an eye on a new suit. The rest Hank planned on saving. That was the first day of delight, and it felt endless.

But time can bring about a change. More days would pass, and Hank's joy began to spoil and crust over because the promised money never made it to his hand, only to his ears: "Soon, boy, soon."

Ollie had been born with a wise soul. Despite her youth, she could read people and signs just as well as some of the elderly women.

And the first sign she read that made her nervous was Hank constantly asking if she'd go away with him.

Doggone your time, Hank. You ah impatient man. You want everything to go like you say, when you say. But life just doesn't always roll out the red carpet like that. And when it doesn't, you get mad as the devil.

Who knew that would be his downfall?

Ollie knew. She had a premonition in the barn. She and Hank were there, relaxing, holding hands, looking out the window at the stars. And that's when Ollie saw it.

"Oh Lord, did you see that, Hank?"

"What?"

"Ah flash in the sky maybe? A burst of something."

"What, one of them shooting stars?"

"Nah, I've seen those before. And they're beautiful. Not this. What I saw was a bad light. It's a sign something's wrong—"

Hank put his hand over Ollie's mouth. "I don't wanna hear nothing about anything bad happening. As much as your daddy can't stand me, he's right about one thing. You hang around Mama Root too much."

"I do not." Ollie pouted. "Not really. She's been awful

good to me and wouldn't do me any harm. She's helping me to read signs."

"Don't you know sometimes you say things and it makes them so? I feel good here with you and that's all that matters. The good."

"And don't I wish that was all there could be to it? Don't you know I want nothing but good between us ever. Think, man."

"I am thinking. Nothing can come 'tween us—except," Hank dropped his voice, "your green-eyed ways."

"Or," Ollie raised her voice and her head, "your wanna-please-everybody ways."

Hank stood up and, half fooling, half joking, demanded to know, "Are we fighters or are we lovers?"

Feeling defiant and flush with contrariness, Ollie cocked her head and shrugged. "Don't rightly know."

"If we fighters," Hank began teasing, "I'll win."

"Is that right?"

"I'll have you know I sit an awful high horse, girl."

"Well," Ollie laughed, "maybe I'm just the low branch you need."

"I'd love it if you took me down a peg," Hank said in a low, stirring voice.

And Ollie kissed him with such passion that when their lips parted he dropped to his knees and was left helpless, gently clutching her hands.

"Hank, get up, man."

"I don't ever wanna stand again in this world and not know for sure that you love me. Do you love me?"

Ollie blushed. "I love you."

"Then come here."

Ollie eased down to her knees in the hay in front of Hank. There, beneath the beams of moonlight that streaked through the cracks in the roof, they held each other with mutual admiration, much in the same way that the stars enjoy the company of the moon. Their desire for each other's happiness burned deep within their souls.

But fate has a way of dousing love's expectations at times that are inconsistent with our highest of hopes.

Two evenings later, Ollie and her father were headed home on their wagon. A young colored boy came riding up like the wind, shouting, "Help! Help!"

Ollie recognized him as one of Hank's helpers on the honey farm.

"Lord, Jesus, Mr. Forester and Penny Less Paul is after Hank something awful. They say he stole some money! He was headed to yo' place, looking for Ollie. They on his trail."

Ollie's father snapped the reins and tore down the road toward their farm. The galloping hooves against the dew-moist ground drummed out a solemn beat that later, when recalled, made Ollie think of the mourners parade she'd seen once during a visit to New Orleans.

When they came into the clearing, they saw Penny Less Paul fighting with Hank. Mr. Forester was sitting on his wagon; a lantern hanging on a nearby hook illuminated his twisted, angry face.

"Hank! Hank!" Ollie called out.

The Hatwearer's Lesson

Hank laid out Penny Less Paul with a right cross and turned and ran into the barn. As Ollie and her father pulled up, they could hear the crossbar being slammed down inside, locking the door.

"Dammit Paul!" Mr. Forester shouted, climbing down off the wagon.

Penny Less Paul growled, "By God, let's burn him out!"

"Hold on there now!" Ollie's daddy shouted, running toward the barn.

Mr. Forester drew a small hand pistol and pointed. "Get on back, Winston. I didn't want it to come to this here but it has."

Then Penny Less Paul began piling brush in front of the barn. He grabbed a bottle of moonshine and soaked the brush. After that Mr. Forester yanked down the lantern and smashed it against the door and the yellow flames belched forward.

"Stop! Oh God, Hank!" Ollie struggled against her father's arms as he held her.

"Terri . . . chile, I was yelling and screaming for dear Jesus. And that fire just grew and grew. And I got so mad that I thought my own brain was on fire inside my head. And just from the stress of it, my heart started beating so fast that I just blacked out, completely."

Terri rocked back. The story had sunk in. "Oh, how awful."

The door to the hospital room opened. "Miss Ollie," a nurse said, entering, "time for your medicine."

She handed Grandma Ollie a small plastic cup with brown liquid in it.

"There's the rum, where's the Coca-Cola?"

"Behave, Miss Ollie. You need your rest if you gonna get better, and I have to change that dressing on your hip."

Terri kissed Grandma Ollie. "I'll call you tonight and see you tomorrow."

"Okay." Grandma Ollie beamed as Terri turned to leave. She told the nurse, "That's my granddaughter. She's an attorney. Better than Johnnie Cochran."

Terri began walking down the hallway. Her thoughts were racing: And I thought I had man troubles. Grandma Ollie saw that? How'd she keep her head?

Terri's cell phone rang. She stopped to pull it out of her belt clip.

"Hello?"

"Hey, baby."

Derek's voice sounded rich and sexy.

"Baby?"

"Yeah." She swallowed, and then glanced down at the diamond engagement ring on her finger.

"You're hard to catch. Every time I call your office Haji says you're in some meeting."

That's what I told her to tell you, Terri thought. She didn't want Derek to know where she was.

"I left messages for you at home too. Meet me now. Where are you?"

"At the pawnshop."

"Pawnshop?"

"Yeah," Terri said real low, "I was trying to see what I could get for this engagement ring. The man said the diamonds were genuine but the promise was a knockoff."

"Oh, you're still being funky."

"Fun-*K* . . . *L-M-N-O* . . . *P*-funk as a matter of fact. What did you think was in the middle of my chest, Derek? Silly Putty that you could just punch and twist, then toss away after you got tired of playing with it?"

"Terri, you know it wasn't like that."

"I've got a heart and it has muscles. You messed me over and only a wimp wouldn't fight back."

"You'd do better if you'd stop fighting so much and start feeling."

"Ain't that nothing? You've got a lot of nerve, Derek. Feelings? You crushed mine."

"And don't you think I hate it? But I'm far from perfect and so are you. I've been thinking—"

"About who you're going to seduce next?"

"See what I mean, Terri? Some of that passion you're pumping into being bitchy should roll over into some forgiveness."

"Because?"

"Goddamnit, because stuff happens, Terri. Okay? You've done the rain dance on a brother's heart before."

"No, I didn't."

"Busted. Remember when we were having brunch a couple of weeks ago at the House of Blues? Ran into one of my frats?"

Terri thought hard: Yeah, but I didn't know him. "That was the first time I ever saw that guy."

"Not quite."

"Please, Derek, don't you think I know who I go out with?"

"Not him. His partner Mel."

Awwww shoot, Terri thought as she pictured Mel. He was sweet as cane sugar. Had to be—all Terri's friends said the boy looked like he was separated at birth from Porky Pig.

Terri had to muster up the words "I liked Mel."

She had just gotten out of a relationship that was raggedy as a poor man's drawers. Mel wasn't handsome but he was nice, a gentleman who gave Terri time to rebound. She did like him—a little bit.

"Mel romanced you with his wallet. Then when you met me, you dumped him," Derek trumpeted. "So you have dogged somebody before. So why are you being so hard on me?"

"What's Winnie up to?" Terri asked, grabbing for some way to hurt Derek.

"I don't know. Maybe I'll call her and find out."

"I hope she's at the hairdresser doing something with that pitiful weave. I've got fuzz balls on my couch that are more bouncing and behaving."

"You know what your problem is, Terri? You think you're perfect. But you're not. Not even close. And you're looking for perfection in everybody around you."

"Then I'm disappointed in myself and in you. In myself for wanting things perfect, because I thought *we* deserved them that way."

"We do, Terri, and dog, we can try if you'll stop grinding up dirt from the past every morning and sipping it like a cup of coffee."

But I don't know if I can trust you again, Terri thought. Can I? She closed her eyes and played with the ring on her finger. Do I want to?

"Terri?"

"I gotta go," she said with as much steel in her voice as she could cast.

"I need to see you. If not now, maybe tonight? If not tonight, then when?"

"No. I don't know when. Soon, maybe."

"Terri, damn, wake up, baby. You're dreaming a fractured fairy tale. I'm not Prince Charming and there are no glass slippers on your feet either. We're two black folks in love, trying to have it going on, and that can be a whole lot if you let it."

A tear began to roll down Terri's cheek. And she wasn't quite sure why she was crying, she had so much to cry about. She felt herself getting weak. She still loved Derek. Terri sniffled.

"You're crying? Baby, please." Derek began to melt. "I—I don't know what's happening to us. Don't cry, Terri. I wish I was there to wipe your tears away."

"No, thanks."

"Terri, Prince Charming is not gonna walk up and hand you a Kleenex okay? Just—"

"Bye, Derek." Terri pressed the end button on her cell phone.

She blindly fumbled with the chrome latch on her Gucci purse.

"Here," a man said as he walked up to Terri in the hospital hallway. He handed her a white hanky. "No more tears."

Tears are liquid emotion; shimmering, pristine, jamming, slamming down a woman's face for joy or laughter, for sorrow or for memories. Terri's tears were for sorrow.

The tear resting now on Grandma Ollie's cheek was for

memories, memories of Hank and the burning barn. She recalled being so distraught that she broke out in a fever, blistering her face, especially the skin around her cheeks, blisters quenched only when the teary river inside her overflowed.

Grandma Ollie remembered now . . . could see herself back then, only sixteen, tears streaming down her face when she awoke and the barn had burned to the ground . . .

Ollie's father cradled her like he used to hold her during their swimming lessons: wading, wading a half a dozen feet into the river.

This is how you swim, Ollie Mae, easy. Let the water do the work. Never fight the water. You can't beat the water.

All right, Daddy.

And when Ollie was able, some five days later, she went up to Lovers Rock to mourn for Hank . . . and there got the surprise of her life.

A surprise she was now sure to tell her granddaughter about, because it was among the lessons she wanted so much for Terri to learn.

Chapter 11

Learning is fundamental, especially when it comes to romance, Terri thought. The breakdown is cleaner than a James Brown split:

Fun as in: the excitement of having a new person come into your life.

Da as in: *Duh, I wonder how this is gonna work out—good, bad, or what was that about?*

Mental as in: *Getting to know you, getting to know all about you.*

What do they like? What do they dislike? What kind of family do they come from? What do they do for a living? What do they do to enjoy themselves?

That's the stuff a person will tell you.

Other things you have to deduce, seduce, and produce out of the experiences you share together.

Terri's legal mind was taught to draw conclusions, to put *two and two together* to determine whether or not to go for it.

Like the white hanky: Her grandfather and the men of that time, the hatwearing, boots-blacked, cuffs-linked, ties-clipped, pants-cuffed, face-shaved, hands-on-the-door-opening-it-for-a-sister era.

That bygone *why is it gone* era.

So when Terri saw the man attached to the white hanky, with the James Earl Jones voice, she thought it could be a close encounter of the most interesting kind.

"My name's Lynnwood Conway."

"Terri Mills."

Fundamentally, Terri took in his smooth dark skin. He had brown eyes, clear and simple in their gaze. A neat 'fro, not more than two inches high, with speckles of light bouncing off the neatly clustered strands. He was clearly a country boy, khaki pants and a checkered shirt, sleeves rolled up; a wink of white from his ribbed T-shirt could be seen above the second open button. Seemed like a nice, regular guy.

Lynnwood appreciated Terri's tears, the fact that her emotions were so full, so sharp that they could spill over in public, and she didn't seem pitiful or shamed. He admired the way she squared her shoulders when offered the hanky, the way she knew enough to accept help yet was proud in how she took it.

"Miss Ollie is your grandmother, right?"

"Right." Terri smiled, then tried to make light of her tears. "Don't suppose you'd let me hang on to this hanky for a while, huh?"

"Keep it." Lynnwood chuckled. "My kitchen sponge is drier."

Terri dabbed at her eyes again.

"I'm with the hospital. They pay me to read to the seniors."

"Oh, that's nice."

"The other day I told Miss Ollie they had a special program for seniors. Before I could go any further, she asked me, 'Is it free?' I said yes. She said, well, whatever it is, put me down for two.' "

Lynnwood laughed and it was infectious. Terri caught it and broke out in a peal of laughter too.

"Now, ain't that better'n all that crying?"

"Sometimes a girl needs a good cry."

"Why? Crying first never changes anything. It just takes up the time you could be using towards figuring out how to fix your problem."

"Maybe the need is in the delay."

"Maybe. What does your grandma like? I read from books mostly. Romance. Mystery. Sci-fi. Biographies."

"Romance."

"I'll bet you like mysteries."

"Why would you bet that?"

" 'Cause you're a mystery to me; a nice woman like you crying in the hallway. Miss Ollie says you're havin' a courting problem."

Terri turned and leaned against the wall. Under her breath she whispered, "I can't believe she told my business like that."

"Sorry, didn't catch that?"

"Never mind," Terri said, surprised at the anger peppering her voice. "I've gotta go."

"Need a ride?"

"No," Terri drawled out, appreciating the kindness, but still brimming with citified caution. "I'll take a cab."

"You found out." Lynnwood turned to the nurses sitting at their station. "Y'all mustah told on me."

"Told what?" one of the nurses questioned.

Lynnwood paused and said seriously, "I'm a serial killer."

Terri's face went blank.

"Every morning without mercy I take out a box of Wheaties and a gallon of milk. I'm dangerous, better not get in the car with me."

The nurses snickered. It was so corny even Terri wanted to laugh, but she held back—although not enough to hide the glint of amusement in her eyes.

"Where's the laugh?" Lynnwood swiveled his head left and right, scanning her face. "There's some more laughter hiding up in there, I know."

Terri refused to budge a muscle.

"Okay, I'm not a greedy man. I'll settle for a smile."

Not a twitch.

Lynnwood stretched his body as tall as it would go and stuck out his chest. "Okay, half a smile or my ego won't hold up. That's the same as a man riding on a flat tire. It's a dangerous thing."

Terri smiled.

"Now, that's a time. My ego's back up to snuff. Let me

take you home. The cab man won't go hungry 'cause he missed your fare."

"Do you offer every woman you meet a ride home?"

"No, only the damsels in distress."

"Grandma Ollie exaggerates," Terri said, walking toward the elevator that would take them to the parking lot.

"Mite. But wasn't that you who was just crying a river in the hallway? I don't know what the standards are in Chicago, Illinois, but that's a sign of Grade A stress down here in Collingswood, Arkansas."

He's got an answer for everything, Terri thought. "Shouldah been a lawyer, Lynnwood."

"Lawyers are cheats. They say one thing and do another. They take and don't give. Wouldn't trust a lawyer to do right even if he was handcuffed to a pole outside the police station."

Terri gave him a wry smile as the elevator began its descent. "That's tough talk."

"I'm for real."

"How many lawyers do you know?"

"One. Messed up a land deal that cost my father some property that had been in our family for years."

"And he or she—"

"He. A woman lawyer probably wouldah really messed it up."

Listen to you, Terri thought, with your sexist butt.

They got off the elevator and began walking through the parking lot.

"If you plan on staying awhile, you might wanna think about renting a car."

"Yeah, I shouldah drove my Beemer."

"Your what?"

"Beemer, BMW 735. I should have drove it but I hate putting all those miles on it."

"Right here."

They stopped in front of a late-model Ford four-by-four truck. After hearing about Terri's fancy automobile, Lynnwood suddenly seemed embarrassed. "It's not what you're used to but I got a good deal on it," he said in an excuse-making tone. "Bought it off the Clampetts after they struck oil and moved to Beverly."

"Hey," Terri said to put Lynnwood at ease, "I'd ride a shooting arrow if it got me from point A to point B.

"You do have a sense of humor." Lynnwood opened the door for Terri. "Thought it might have drowned in all those tears."

"In tough times, a sense of humor floats."

Lynnwood shut the truck door.

Alone in the truck, Terri said to herself, "Brains I'm not so sure about, with all the mistakes I've been making lately."

She was quiet during the ride home, just thinking, thinking what to do about Derek and their relationship.

Lynnwood glanced at her from time to time, deciding it best to leave her be despite the fact that there was so much he wanted to ask this woman. She had a quality about her that he hadn't seen before. Lynnwood stole another glance at Terri.

She was a handsome woman, as his father would say, and his father before him; her strong features and soft, shiny hair attracted him but didn't intrigue him.

So what had put Lynnwood in the mind to chase?

It was the look in Terri's eyes when she talked; clearly a mind was racing behind those big brown eyes, examining you and what you said, but somehow without being intimating or judgmental. It seemed tricky as hell, Lynnwood reasoned. Like pulling a rabbit out of a hat. The hat is real. The rabbit is real. The mechanics of how it's done is what stumps you.

"Thanks for the ride, Lynnwood."

"Sure thing."

As soon as Terri got out of the car, her cousin Sugar came running to the front door.

"Terri," she yelled, holding up the phone. "You got a call. From Chicago. It's your law office."

Lynnwood's mouth dropped faster than a bucket falling down a well.

Terri bent down and teased through the open window. "Now that your mouth's open, why don't you take your foot out?"

Terri laughed to herself as she jogged to the front door to take the receiver from Sugar. "This is Terri . . . Haji, whoa, wait a minute. Talk slow."

The news made Terri weak in the knees. Gravity did the rest. She plopped down on the padded bench nearest the door. A heavy sigh billowed from her chest. Terri closed her eyes.

Haji said over the phone, "It's hit the fan."

"And splattered all over the wall," Terri responded.

Whenever Terri saw a mess, she always felt she had to clean it up. Even in the first grade, some other child would leave the blocks scattered all over the floor, and Terri would be the one to put them back up. The girl just couldn't stand to walk away from a mess.

Neither could the woman.

But this time the mess wasn't just splattered on the wall—it was splattered all over her career too.

Baxter & Associates had made an aboveboard request: The lawyers wanted the city to give them more time to explore new information that would help their negligence case.

Of course, Terri and her legal crew said no.

The below-board leverage was that the lead attorney had heard that Terri sandbagged a paralegal who once worked on the case at Baxter & Associates but who was now with another firm. Was it payback for the Baxter case? Could be improper enough to make a stink, but not bad enough that it couldn't be overlooked if B&A got this little favor.

That paralegal was Zelda.

"Okay, Haji, tell me: Who over at B and A is making this a bigger mess than the Valdez oil slick?"

"Crenshaw."

Of course: the man with the heart two sizes too small. Who else would stop at nothing to get the upper hand? Who else was known as the Ty Cobb of litigation? Known for flying into other lawyers spikes-high. Dirty as the bottom of a rusty washtub. Smart as Bill Gates on Gingkoba.

"Call his bluff, Terri. I know you didn't sandbag this woman, that's not your style."

No time for secrets. Terri was about to go to war and Haji was going to be in the foxhole with her. So Terri told her that she did sandbag Zelda, because her heart was torn apart. Wouldn't any woman lash out? It was a professional drive-by only because Terri was now firmly a part of the black upper class; she was beyond kicking off her pumps, taking out her earrings, and greasing down her face with Vaseline for a *ghetto claw brawl*.

It was personal revenge, not professional sabotage. Terri had no idea that Zelda had worked at B&A, let alone had logged time on the city's big case. What Terri had done was simple; she made a common mistake and had taken out her anger on the wrong person. She was paying for it too—got her tires slashed and now Zelda was taking a stab at her rep.

But now it was time to stop paying.

"Hang tough. I'll keep you in the loop." Terri hung up with Haji.

Then Terri sent a 9-1-1 page to her friend Niecy, the one who had blackballed Zelda at the job.

"Look, girl, this thing is out of control. Zelda slashed my tires, now she's gone to the boys at Baxter and Associates trying to mess up a case I'm working on."

"I'm sorry, Terri. Zelda found out about the bad recommendation I gave her through my big-mouthed secretary. She didn't mean any harm, just wanted to give her girlfriend an FYI, like I was trying to take care of you. Trust me, she won't do that again."

"I'm sorry I got you involved in the first place."

"Forget about it. The least I can do is help you fix it. Anything you need, just let me know, Terri."

"Can you get me a private number for Zelda? A cell phone, no in-house line."

Niecy went into the interoffice phone list, pulled a number, and gave it to Terri. She dialed it immediately.

"This is Zee."

"Zelda, this is Terri Mills."

"Hi, bitch."

Gutter-mouth tactics. Ticky-tack stuff. Terri had played rough and tough with the best of them. She shook off that little slur like a speck of dandruff on a black sweater.

"Zelda, you have every right to be mad. I took you out of an opportunity for something you didn't do."

"C'mon. C'mon with it, girl."

"But stop and think. How did I get to that place? You work around lawyers all day, hear and see cases. You were letting your backbone slip east and west, always grinding on someone else's man, husband, or fiancé in public—constantly. That's why the evidence loved you the best."

"It takes two to grind, Terri."

"And two to rumble. But here's the deal. I'm willing to walk away and call it a draw—"

"Bitch, please. I'm not through with you. I've got B and A on your behind."

"And I'll have the police on yours."

"For what?"

"For slashing my tires."

"The police won't want to be bothered with a bunch of piddly stuff like that."

"Not if you had done it in front of my house. But you did it in a private garage, Zelda. That's criminal trespassing all day long."

"No one saw me."

"The biggest and best eye belongs to the video camera. Plus you wrote a note—unable to get back at a sister without taking a bow. I kept the note. A conviction for criminal trespassing won't land you any jail time if this is your first offense. Just probation. But I know your firm is not going to want someone with a record on staff. Now you're out of a job. So you go looking. Zelda, every job asks have you been convicted of a crime. You'll get turned down more than the sheets on a motel bed."

Terri heard Zelda breathing.

"I was wrong and I'm sorry I started it. You got me back with the tire deal. Let's drop it now. Pull Baxter and Associates; go tell Crenshaw right now that it was personal and not anything to do with the city's case."

"If I wanted to tell him, I couldn't—he's on vacation for two weeks. What am I supposed to do, hunt him down on vacay 'cause your sorry butt is on the line? Get real."

"Then you have two weeks to think about it. You don't want to throw down with me, girl. I've got more power and more contacts than you. Plus I don't like to lose—and I won't lose. But as God is my witness I don't want to go there."

For several seconds not a mumbling word was said by either woman.

Terri shattered the silence. "Good. I can tell you're thinking about it already. Bye."

"Every good-bye ain't gone," Zelda huffed back.

Chapter 12

"G'on 'way from here with that worried look on your face, chile!" Grandma Ollie hooted. "You make sick folks in here look like they work for the Board of Health."

Terri walked into the hospital room followed by Sugar. Terri fell across the bed, giving her grandmother a bear hug. "You are the signifying queen."

Sugar waited her turn, and then hugged Grandma Ollie. "Hey, old lady." Then she stepped back. "How you like my new look?"

Sugar had needed a change so she cut her hair to about three inches in length all around. Then she teased the top and slicked it down on the sides. She had on a red and white striped dress with spaghetti straps as she spun around.

"Honestly?" Grandma Ollie asked.

"Oh Lord," Terri wheezed.

"That dress is too dang tight—you look like a two-liter bottle of Coca-Cola."

Sugar smirked. "Big is beautiful." She had grown up around Grandma Ollie and her mama and took everything they said with a pinch of salt. "You and Mama were always prudish when it came to the body."

"Ain't no prude, just stingy. I like to save something for the imagination. And about your head—Sugar, you got such pretty hair, why cut it so short?"

"Tell her, Terri. Short is in."

"It is, Grandma."

"Okay, okay," Grandma Ollie said, squinting. "It's cute. But what ya rolling it with, matches?"

Terri's knees buckled as she laughed. Sugar joined in with some suave. "Oh, see you wrong. Real wrong."

Terri picked up Grandma Ollie's hand and kissed it. "How ya feeling this morning?"

"Fair to middling. Had a tough night sleeping. I catch winks better in my own bed. But you don't look like you fared much better. Worried about Derek?"

Terri didn't want to burden Grandma Ollie with her work drama so she hesitated before answering. Sugar jumped in. "Yep, sure is."

"I knew it. Girl, men are like TV commercials: They'll tell you anything and ain't none of it true."

"Stop." Terri pulled a chair up to the side of the hospital bed. "There are some good things about Derek."

"Didn't say there weren't. He's just what I call a crystal man— he looks fine but after a while you can see right through him."

Sugar was standing by the door, distracted. "There are some good-looking doctors up here, Cousin Ollie. I'm gonna take a stroll . . . You convince my little cuz to dump her man while I try to land me one."

Terri sucked wind. "That girl is so fast."

"Can't imagine what side of the family she gets it from." Grandma Ollie rolled her eyes then thumped her chest with her index finger before grinning. Then she became serious. "Terri, whatcha figuring on doing about that boy?"

"Tell me what happened after the barn burned down."

"You making a bed you gonna have to lie in—*so don't try to change the sheets.* I wanna talk about you. Turn me an answer."

"I don't know what I'm going to do about Derek. I'm tired of thinking about him. I'm tired of thinking about the mistakes I make in my relationships, period."

"Terri, we're not perfect. That's why we have a savior."

"I don't think God wants to hear about my man problems."

"If you're at the end of your rope—whatever kindah rope it is—ask God to lend you a hand."

"Excuse me, ladies." Lynnwood was now standing in the doorway with one hand behind his back. "Sugar told me you were here, Terri."

"Hi."

Lynnwood smiled then ducked his head toward the hospital bed. "Miss Ollie."

"Mr. Lynnwood—came to eyeball my pretty granddaughter, huh?"

Terri bucked her eyes: *Grandma!*

"Well, everybody's acting all shy. I was just trying to liven things up is all. My goodness, have me arrested by the *keep quiet po-leece,* why don'tcha."

Terri whispered to herself good-naturedly, "Like even a gun and a badge could keep you out of my business."

"Whatcha say?" Grandma Ollie sat up in the hospital bed.

Lynnwood stepped forward and handed Terri a box of chocolate sweets. "I'm sorry about yesterday."

"What'd you do?"

Terri squeezed Grandma Ollie's arm. "Nothing. Don't you wanna watch TV or something?"

"Chile, you and your goings-on are better than any soap opera."

Lynnwood laughed.

Terri cut her eyes at him and thought, Don't encourage her.

"Terri," Lynnwood said. "The candy is part one of my apology. Part two is I'd like to invite you to Bible study tonight. It's for singles and usually we have a lot of cool discussions. It's fun."

"Hmmm." Terri tugged slightly at her ear. It would be a way to get out of the house. She pointed at her pantsuit. "Plan on being here most of the day. I won't have time to change—is this okay?"

"Sure it—"

"Nooooooo!" Grandma Ollie hooted. "Don't you wear pants to church. That's a black mark—and God's gonna blame that on me as if I didn't teach you any better. And ya know I'm going before you."

Terri became extremely demonstrative. "Can you pick me up after Sugar drops me off at home to change?"

"I do believe that would be the highlight of my day."

Little did Terri know that it would be the highlight of her day too.

She enjoyed the Bible study class and met some other folks from Collingswood; all of them knew Grandma Ollie. She had advised someone's mother or was a playmate of someone's grandma.

But being with Lynnwood was fun and easy. He had a wonderful sense of humor, often cracking the best jokes at just the right time. Terri even got in a few good ones here and there, realizing at that moment how important laughter is to the spirit.

"That was fun," Terri said as Lynnwood walked her to the door afterward.

"You dialed it up a notch." Lynnwood's stroll was slow and steady. "I think some of those small-town girls were trying to impress a city woman like yourself with their ideas."

"Most women have the same idea when it comes to a relationship and how it fits in with our religious lives."

"Oh, and what's that?"

"Weren't you listening?"

Lynnwood leaned against the door. "Yep. But I just wanna hear you speak on it. I'm enjoying your company. I'm trying to be in it for as long as I can."

Terri felt herself blush and was so glad that it was dark so Lynnwood couldn't see. "Women want a man who believes in God and the vows of marriage—loyalty, honesty, providing . . ."

"And men really want to do those things for women. They do."

Terri nodded intently. She thought of Derek. "Even loyalty before marriage, when they're still dating?"

Lynnwood stood flat-footed. "When a man finds the woman he really loves, the one he respects and wants to call wife, there is nothing on earth he won't do for her. No mountain he won't hike. No river he won't wade. No door he won't open. She is his Eve and there's not a snake crawling that can keep them apart."

Terri smiled. "Sounds good. But can women really believe in romance like that nowadays?"

"If they take a cue from *The Wizard of Oz*."

"Like what?"

"Like believing in themselves the way Dorothy did . . . Like using their minds to dream big dreams like the Scarecrow, like having the heart to love without fear like the Tin Man, and the courage to put everything on the line like the Lion."

"Then what?" Terri asked, intrigued.

"Whatcha think?" Lynnwood said, walking backward into the night. "There's no place like love." Then he vanished into the darkness.

Chapter 13

Grandma Ollie was gone.

Terri had brought flowers, a bouquet of red, white, and yellow roses. Grandma Ollie liked roses as much as she did.

But the hospital bed was empty.

The sight frightened Terri so much that she shook violently; so violently that some of the petals flew into the air and wafted down. It looked like someone had SCUD missiled a rainbow and the colorful shrapnel from it was sailing through the air.

The hospital blinds were closed.

With sunlight barred from the room, the area seemed small, bland, and cold. Terri's heart lurched.

The naked bed caught her eye.

Where is she? What's going on? The get-well cards were gone. The fruit basket the church sent was gone. The hand-held mirror she liked to primp in, gone. And in the time that Terri stood there in the empty hospital room worrying, she had a flashback. A reexperience . . .

It was early summer, a very warm day outside. Terri was only ten years old. She scratched at the itchy dime-sized mosquito bites that lined her knees just below the cutoff shorts she wore. Terri also had on her favorite candy-striped tank top, the one she liked so much that she never got tired of fiddling with the droopy straps. No telling which kept her busier, the lazy straps or helping Grandma Ollie around the backyard of their modest brick bungalow.

Terri could see all the other backyards down the block while glancing over the short chain-link fences. The lawns were kept trimmed to perfection, not by gardeners, but by the hands that paid the mortgage, picked up the newspaper, and planted flowers next to the garages out back.

Grandma Ollie and Terri were out back this day, planting tomatoes and green peppers in the backyard. It was a good backyard. It was wide enough to hold a slide that Terri could fly down with abandon and still land on grass, and long enough to hang a clothesline.

Grandma Ollie had a system working. She dug the holes and placed. Terri was the cover-up-dirt packer.

"Mash the soil around the plant good, mash it good and hard with the flat of your hands," Grandma Ollie instructed.

While mashing, Terri had a question that she had been dying to ask, so finally she spoke up. "How do you know God is in heaven?"

Grandma Ollie sucked air. "I just do."

"But you can't see him, so how do you know?"

"I just do!"

"But I don't get it."

"Keep mashing and talk less. Don't it look like rain?"

Terri looked up at the sky and saw a growing patch of gray cloud cover moving swiftly toward the sun.

Time crept along . . . *Mash. Mash. Mash.*

Then Grandma Ollie, without looking in Terri's direction, or at any other place other than where she was digging, asked easily, "Is there a sun?"

"Yes," Terri answered immediately without question.

"Are you sure?"

"Yes."

"Look up."

Terri looked up and saw nothing but the gray cloud cover.

"There's no sun. You can't see it."

"But I know it's there," Terri blurted out. "I can't see it but I can feel it. I know it's there."

"And that's just how God is," Grandma Ollie said, still digging and placing. "You can't see him but you know he's there because you can feel him."

And in that instant the concept of faith crystallized for her. The memory of that now steadied Terri, and finally after what seemed like an eternity she breathed again. As Terri's burdened shoulders rose and fell with each breath, she glanced down the hospital hallway. Lynnwood was now striding toward her with confident steps.

"Come with me," he said, wrapping his arm around Terri's shoulder, helping to pull her back to life.

Lynnwood's voice was strong, calming. He smelled like an inexpensive but manly aftershave. "Your grandmother had to have emergency surgery."

"Why? What was wrong? Is she in surgery now?"

"Don't know. Can't guess. And yes, she's still in surgery. Don't you worry." Lynnwood squeezed Terri's shoulder. "C'mon. I know where we can get some straight answers."

Lynnwood took Terri to the floor where Grandma Ollie was having surgery. They found her doctor there. Terri rushed toward him.

"Doc, what's wrong?"

"The plate rubbed against some bone and caused some bleeding. We had a problem with a clot."

"A blood clot can kill a person," Terri whispered.

"That's why we took Miss Ollie right to surgery. We have a hip specialist here. They're almost done. It's going well so far—but I always like to tell the family to be prepared for the worst. God forbid, at her age the heart can give out at any time."

"No!" It was an affirmation from Terri, not a statement.

"Doc," Lynnwood said. "You're talking about Miss Ollie. From what I can tell, Miss Ollie ain't near about ready to leave here. That is unless it's to go to the Summer Social. Think I'll go myself this year and shake a leg with her."

Terri said thoughtfully to Lynnwood, "She likes to bop."

Lynnwood smiled at Terri then turned to the doctor. "The bop it is."

They were making it clear: There wasn't gonna be a syllable of negative talk about Grandma Ollie not making it. The doctor understood and left quietly. Terri sat down and Lynn-wood joined her. For the first time Terri noticed he had a backpack slung over his shoulder. Her gaze stayed there only a moment, then wafted over to the double doors. Behind them, the most important person to her soul was fighting for survival. Terri closed her eyes and said a prayer. Then she started praying with her eyes wide open.

"Let me read to you, Terri. That'll keep you from worry-ing so much; might even help the time pass faster."

Did she hear? Terri was silent, the blood pumping inside her head, throbbing.

Then Lynnwood's voice began to break through a fence of fear inside of her. He read to her poetry written by Nikki Giovanni.

And before Terri knew it, more than an hour had passed. And the last thing she heard was a duet of voices.

One from a surgeon, "Your grandmother will be fine."

The other from Lynnwood as he read from "Kidnap Poem."

But Lynnwood wasn't a poet, he was just a simple man; he wanted her to come along willingly. Lynnwood vowed to himself to be there for Terri, a friend who could, if the saints allowed, be something more.

Meanwhile Terri's world had become a colander; everything was shifting and separating itself out like yolks from egg whites. Sometimes you have to leave yourself to find yourself. Her love for Derek separated from her fear of their relationship's failure.

Her demand for a superior career separated from her desire for professional respect.

Her adoration for Grandma Ollie separated from her fear of one day being without her.

The shifting and separating began that evening. The sun was setting. Terri had been allowed to see Grandma Ollie briefly after surgery. She was weak but she smiled and managed to squeeze Terri's hand.

Lynnwood waited for Terri until the visiting hours were over and took her home. She offered him pink lemonade. Lynnwood accepted and they went and sat in the backyard, on the old bench swing.

All things in pieces can be meshed together as one. They shared silence first: silence from the sky that was putting the day to bed; the quiet time needed to help put to bed the turmoil that Terri had just been through, and that Lynnwood, practically a stranger, had found it in his heart to step up and steady her through.

Just as ships sail on tumultuous waters, our lives are vessels that get rocked and rolled by people and events. Terri was feeling just about sunk. How much can a person take? How tight can the squeeze be? How bad can the down and dirty get?

Wearily, and without thinking, she rested her head on Lynnwood's shoulder. How natural and beautiful life can be when one person can find comfort in another without thinking. He felt safe. He felt open. So it was there that Terri rested her head and let the tears fall.

And when Lynnwood patted her back and began to pat his pockets looking for something to dry her tears, it was fitting that Terri fish out of her purse the hanky he had loaned her and use it to dry her eyes. Lynnwood cupped the hand that clutched the hanky, then lifted it and kissed her fingers softly, before letting their hands fall back down together on his lap.

That was the inception of possibility.

Chapter 14

"Is it possible that she's that coldhearted?" Haji demanded to know over the phone.

"I thought not," Terri sighed. She was sure that Zelda would withdraw her complaint and call it even. Instead, the longer Zelda thought about it, the madder and more determined she seemed to become. It was becoming clear to Terri that her job mess was about to get messier.

"You might have to fly back to clear this up," Haji said, and sounded as frustrated as Terri felt.

"Let's hope it doesn't come to that. God, I'd hate to have to leave now."

"But if you don't address it in person when it hits, everybody around here will be talking all kinds of junk. You know that."

"I know. I've still got a little time. Grandma Ollie always says patience is a virtue."

Terri was determined to figure out a way to save face, to settle the case before the B&A boys could go to Morgan. She pored over every document on the case. Terri burned the candle at both ends until the flames met in the center. Still her mind came up blank on the solution end. Before she knew it, it was time to go to the hospital.

Grandma Ollie was sitting up, frowning at her lunch. It was chicken soup, a roll, sugar-free Jell-O, and two cartons of skim milk.

"Pitiful!" Grandma Ollie said, shaking her head.

"Doesn't look so bad to me. It's slimming."

"The doctor says my butt is too big." Grandma Ollie played with the soup. "I told him that was 'cause I was sittin' on it."

"He just wants you to watch what you eat."

"I'm looking at it and I don't like what I see. Doc says I've got to listen to my body."

"Good advice."

"My body says Kentucky Fried Chicken."

Terri laughed. "Well, don't listen to that."

"I'm so hungry my body's talking in foreign languages."

"What?"

"Saying Häagen-Dazs and whatnot. Baby, would ya—"

"Sneak you in some ice cream? No ma'am."

"Well, what took you so long to get here today?"

"Job stuff."

"I don't like it when you let that job worry you. I almost liked it better when black folks didn't have all them high-profile jobs. You did an honest day's work, went home, and concentrated on your family. Now y'all career men and women worry more about your bonuses than you do 'bout your babies."

Terri pulled up a chair and sat by Grandma Ollie. "I'm just trying to do right, one step at a time, just like you always taught me. But sometimes it's so hard—"

"Terri, there are things that will happen to you that don't seem possible, that don't seem real. There are things that'll hurt and you think it'll never get better. Some things you just have to do and see for yourself and can't nobody else do it for you. That's just life. Seems like more trouble than it's worth sometimes, feels like it's harder than it needs to be. But you gotta put one foot in front of the other and set things on course."

"That's so easy to say but a hell of a lot harder to pull off."

Grandma Ollie sucked wind. "Don't I know it. But the very first time I realized that was some sixty years ago heading up to Lovers Rock after the barn burning and Hank's funeral . . ."

The climb up Lovers Rock set Ollie's young bones to aching. The aching only matched the pain in her heart. It was a cloudy day, a good day Ollie figured to go, because the brooding sky matched her sorry mood.

How could the man she loved be taken away from her so cruelly? Ollie's faith was strong; never had the foolishness in her to ever doubt God, not even a little bit.

Lord, she thought, I'm not a doubter. But I am wondering what to make of all this. Why can't I have the things I want? I wanted to be with Hank and now he's gone. I found love and wanted to keep that love and now it's gone. Why can't I have the things I want? Lord, I'm hurting and how, how can I stop it?

Ollie would learn that the important questions like that which we ask ourselves can be answered only in our hearts. Not in brittle bird bones rubbed together and rolled out on a person's swaddling cloth.

That was Mama Root's way. She dried the bones of a sparrow that died at her door, claiming God sent the bird to her so she'd be able to give folks direction in their lives. Mama Root asked for a person's birth wrap, the cloth a baby was swaddled in after coming into the world. It made her vision clearer, helped her see inside the soul.

Ollie had the blue, red, and yellow swaddling cloth draped over her arm as she ran, ran to Mama Root's whitewashed shack on the edge of the Glory Woods. Didn't tell her daddy where she went. Oh no. He'd be fit to be tied. Ollie ran forward, clutching the cloth, the air wet and grabby against her skin like a cold hand, trying to stop her, trying to slow her down.

But still Ollie ran.

Her feet seemed so swift, so fleet that the damp red clay barely took form and there was no proof that she had traveled this path.

And why?

Why was nature fighting her destiny? No footprints in the clay. No wind at her back. No relief for her aching soul.

Mama Root swore that she knew the answers. The devil didn't want Ollie to have relief. The wreckage from the barn burning still smoldered in back of her house. Ollie smelled it at night. Inhaled it in the morning. Mama Root said it wouldn't stop smoldering because Ollie's love still burned and she would have to say good-bye to Hank for good to put out the smoldering embers and the sorrow in her heart.

But how?

"Do exactly as I say and don't change nary a thing," Mama Root advised.

So Ollie had to make the journey, go up to Lovers Rock without Hank. She took a scarf Hank had given her, a comb, a toenail clipper, and ashes from the barn.

Ollie carefully spread out the scarf, then turned her dress pocket inside out, dumping the ashes on top. Then she washed her hair in the river, let it get soaked with water till the heaviness made her neck feel like it would break. Then Ollie washed her feet; soaked them until the roundness of her heels wrinkled up like a bowl of prunes.

Then Ollie began to comb her hair, and that which was dead, shed itself, falling. Then she began to clip her toenails, slivers falling. Most of it fell on the scarf. Then Ollie sat quietly and waited.

Mama Root had said to wait; wait till the sun lit the edge of the sky just above the river and the water caught fire and burned orange. When the orange blaze grew and enflamed the entire sky, Ollie was to burn the scarf and everything in it.

Time brings about a change, the minister had preached at Hank's graveside. Time. A young man's life taken too soon: stolen by prejudice, buried in injustice.

The sheriff had said, "The boy was a thief. A thief gets what he gets."

Ollie couldn't have said she was standing there at the graveside. She was planted there. Her spirit grew roots, roots grounded in sorrow.

Time would bring about a change, the minister said. A change for the better because Hank was now in God's place.

Time would bring about a change, the minister said. At some point Ollie would no longer ache from head to toe because Hank was gone.

As these graveside memories flared up in Ollie's brain, the sun struck the edge of the sky at dusk and the blaze began. When the burning in the sky seemed as intense as the burning in her heart, Ollie closed her eyes and said a prayer for relief.

That was Ollie's idea, not Mama Root's.

Ollie opened her eyes and began to do as instructed. She shook the edge of the scarf, and the hair and the toenail clippings fluttered to the center mixed in with the ashes. Ollie reached into her dress pocket and pulled out a tiny box of matches. Her hands were trembling. Ollie had struck the match and leaned her body forward, when a huff blew out the flame.

It was not the wind.

It was a breath, Hank's breath.

Ollie drew on every power in her body: the blood, the nerves, the fear, and the awe. These things kept her from screaming until she fainted.

Barely conscious, Hank took her in his arms. "Baby, I'm sorry. Wasn't trying to scare you. You okay?"

Ollie's eyes focused, her hands clenched around Hank's

upper arms, feeling skin and bones, making sure this was no ghost. Then she dug her nails into his flesh.

"Awww!"

Then Ollie reached for a branch that the wind had broken from a tree. She grabbed it and hit Hank with it.

"Wait a minute!" Hank said, jumping up running. "Wait!"

"I'm gonna beat the living daylights out of you."

Hank scampered up the nearest tree, half laughing. "I didn't know you was so ornery."

"Get down from there!"

"If I didn't know any better, Ollie, I'd swear you didn't love me. How you gonna beat on the one you love?"

"We done cried for you, done prayed for you, and done buried you. I'm determined to see that folks ain't disappointed." She whacked the tree trunk with the stick. "Get your chicken behind out of that tree. You act like you don't have good sense."

"I don't when it comes to you, Ollie. Lookah here," Hank said, flapping his arms like a chicken. "Putting the cluck on just for you."

As funny as Hank looked, a giggle surely grew in Ollie's gut. But by the time the giggle channeled itself up through her tormented soul, it came out in chuckles that dissolved into a passel of tears. Ollie dropped to her knees and cried softly into her palms.

Hank flowed down from the tree with the ease of a spirit and settled around Ollie's shoulders. She wanted to shake him off but hadn't the strength or the mind to. All she could mumble was "Where you been, man? Where you been?"

Hank clutched Ollie tighter, stroked her wet hair that smelled sweet from windblown petals that had gotten swept into the river. "Sssh, now, sssh."

Ollie wanted to get lost in the warmth of Hank's body; she tried to melt herself into it, bond with it, and lather herself all over with his touch. After several long moments, Hank explained.

"Had to do it, Ollie. You know I've been telling you that Mr. Forester's been cheating me. I got tired of it. So I just took what was mine."

"You did steal that money?"

"Are you listening?" Hank said, turning Ollie's chin toward his own face. "I took what was mine."

"But the fire, how'd you get out of the barn?"

"I wasn't the only one old man Forester was cheating. He was cheating Penny Less Paul too. A poor white man ain't but one step above a colored to a man like Mr. Forester. Dogged him just about as much as he did me. That's why we were friends even though Mr. Forester tried to turn him against me. But we both knew he'd never do right by either one of us."

"So?"

"So Penny Less Paul broke into the wall safe. How'd I ever get close enough to Mr. Forester to get the combination? Paul could though. I saw him through the window, stealing the money."

"And just like that you decided to go in on it together?"

"He knew I could tell on him; maybe folks would believe me or maybe they wouldn't. It would still cast a doubt on him, no matter what. Or Penny Less Paul could blame it on me, which is more than likely what the law would take as gospel. Ollie, it was like we were reading each other's mind. Wasn't but one good way out for the both of us."

Ollie shook her head.

"We throwed in with each other. I came up with the plan. Penny Less Paul would ask Mr. Forester for an advance, and when the old man went to the safe and saw the money gone— he'd tell Mr. Forester I had been in there."

"How'd they know where to find you?"

"I told Paul I would be on the way to your place; all part of the plan. Mr. Forester does dirty but he never gets the mess on his own hands. I knew he would have Penny Less Paul come in after me. See I'd come to the barn earlier. I dug a hole out from under the back, hid it on the inside with hay. So when Penny Less Paul set the fire, I sneaked out the back and ran. Everybody would think I was dead. Later, we met up at a secret place to divide the money."

Ollie balled up her hands to keep from slapping his face. "And you put me and my daddy at risk like that? How could you?"

"I ain't do that. Remember," Hank said, taking Ollie in his arms. "Remember you told me y'all would be gone overnight to your aunt's. You came back early."

Ollie sighed at the truth. Then she shrugged. "Now what? You in worse shape than before. You got your money but no job. You can't come back. Whatcha gonna do?"

"I'm leaving. You know I've been wanting to leave."

"Hank, you'd say that every time you lost at cards; when you won, you'd talk about marriage."

"Well, use the brain God gave you, girl," Hank said with a low stirring voice. "I can't possibly stay. I gotta go. And the only reason I'm still here is because of you."

Ollie's body convulsed. He wants me to run away with him, she thought. I love him, but that'll break Daddy's heart.

"Come with me, Ollie."

"I don't know. This is too much to think about at one time. I thought you were gone and now you're back. Running away with you will break my daddy's heart."

"You can't keep hanging on to your daddy's suspenders forever. I know your mama died in childbirth and your sister passed away. I'm sorry for all that. But you gotta grow up sometime, Ollie."

"And you figure you've got the magic say-so over when and how?"

Hank searched Ollie's face. Then he pulled her close. "If you gonna be with me Ollie, you have to see things like I see them. That money was owed me. And I'm gonna give you some money to pay for your daddy's barn."

Ollie dropped her head, distraught.

Hank lifted her chin. "But hear me now. I love you and I want you with me, but yes or no, I gotta go. Tell me, whatcha gonna do, girl? And please don't make a mountain out of a molehill."

Chapter 15

Contemporary thought says don't make something out of nothing and don't sweat the small stuff. Right now, in Terri's life, none of it was small stuff. She grappled with what to do about her relationship with Derek. This unexpected journey down south was the circumstance that had provided her with space—space to think.

When our heart is involved, our brain doesn't always act like it has good sense. We wrestle with emotions, flip-flopping as if we're trying to pin an enemy when we're simply trying to get ahold of our true selves.

Terri knew the things that she loved about Derek—his smarts, his cool, his up-and-coming ways. But now she was like a famed astronomer who from a distance can marvel at things discovered.

In her distance from Derek, she looked back and marveled

at the number of times that he had disappeared on the weekends, only to emerge to say that he'd been in consultant hell with a client.

She marveled at how often Derek had taken trips to hang out with his brother, but when she had called, he never answered his cell until he was about to come home. Terri had been so busy herself with work that she never questioned these absences. Now she did.

Was Derek working all of those times? Was he with other women? Was Winnie an isolated case?

Derek was the biggest flirt she had ever dated. Terri chalked it up to him flexing his charm. Who had she ever met with an abundant charm who didn't overuse it? Terri knew she was just fronting on herself. She knew Derek was a huge flirt, and there's not a true flirt in the world—man or woman—that might not follow through on those impulses at least once.

Now that Terri was able to meditate on their relationship, she tried to analyze how Derek made her feel. When they made love, it was solitary bliss. They had chemistry together, but now Terri wondered if they would continue to have history together.

Outside of their lovemaking, Terri felt comfortable with Derek but never *really good* with Derek. It was a crazy thing, she discovered now. She felt like they were always on the go, showcasing themselves as a couple. Always on. At the mixers. At the fund-raisers. At the cocktail parties. Always the "couple's couple." They would go from showcasing to lovemaking: intense to *really intense*. Terri hadn't realized there was a gap until now.

When she mentioned this fact to Grandma Ollie, the old diva commented, *You never know there's a hole in your pocket until something falls through.*

And what hit the ground and made a loud thud was the concept of *ease.* Terri had perpetual excitement with Derek but never ease. She wouldn't even know what ease felt like if it were not for Lynnwood.

Lynnwood was ease personified. It was the way he told a joke and the way he smiled. It was the way he walked. It was the way he was around you, like he belonged and would be out of place anywhere else.

Ease was the way Terri would describe how Lynnwood sat on a horse. He loved horses. Lynnwood took Terri to a corral where he and some of his other rodeo buddies kept their animals.

Lynnwood's favorite horse was a filly named Princess.

"I named her that and all my friends talked about me like a dog. But I didn't care. She had the most beautiful gait of any horse I'd ever seen. She had power and grace. Wasn't nothing else fitting her but the name Princess."

And the horse was as beautiful as Lynnwood described. One evening, near the end of dusk, Lynnwood took Terri to see Princess. The horse's copper brown coat was as glistening as the setting sun. Her face was full and she held her head high. Lynnwood extended his hand and Princess moved forward steadily and gently. Lynnwood motioned with his head toward Terri, who stood next to him. "Give her a kiss, Princess."

And the horse snuggled her nose against the side of Terri's

face. Terri had never been so relaxed before, here with the
cool evening breeze, with the smell of wildflowers, with a
horse that gave kisses, and with a man who had no agenda
other than to spend some quiet time with her.

Ease.

Terri found herself looking forward to going with Lynnwood once in a while to feed Princess. The horse now began
to bray a loud hello whenever she saw Terri.

"We like you a lot," Lynnwood said. And it was easy, no
pressure behind it, like they should be more than what they
were, which was two people enjoying each other's company.

One night Terri sat up in bed. She didn't know what woke
her but she knew what was bothering her. She grabbed her
cell phone and dialed Derek's number. When he clicked on
the phone, Terri could hear the loud music in the back-
ground.

"Terri? I'm so glad you called. I've been thinking about
you . . ."

Yeah, Terri thought, you're really bummed out over our
problems—out enjoying yourself at a big old party.

"Derek, I need to ask you something—"

"What?"

"I need to ask you something!"

"Wait . . . let me go where I can hear better . . ."

Terri waited until the music became faint and the hum of
an occasional car going by could be heard. "Is that better,
Terri?"

"Yes . . ."

"Listen, baby, we've—"

Terri blurted out, "Name me one time we were together and we did nothing but hold each other."

"Huh?"

Terri brought her knees to her chest and wrapped one arm around them and began to rock. "I said name me one time you and I were together and we did nothing but hold each other."

"Uh . . . uh . . ."

"I couldn't think of any time either. And you know what? That's a problem, Derek."

"Wait a minute. This is some new stuff you're throwing at me. Ain't the old drama enough? I don't understand what you're trying to get at."

"What are we feeling when we're not together making the world sit up and take notice or making love?"

"Well . . . we—we feel love."

"Derek, you answered that like a kid who just got called on in class."

" 'Cause you asked the question like it was a pop quiz."

Terri's toes curled up. "How do you know we feel love if we've never shared that moment? How do we know that we are even at ease with each other? We're talking about growing old together . . ."

"Terri—"

"And what happens after the careers and the kids and when the sex drive drops off ? . . ."

"Terri—"

"Will we be content enough in just each other? In the comfort that we have with one another?"

"Terri . . . you're tripping. I love you and you love me. Everybody says we're the perfect couple. Don't mess with perfection."

"Perfection is in the eye of the beholder."

Chapter 16

"Terri, you are a welcome sight to behold. You know your grandma has climbed up the rough side of the mountain and now I'm sliding down the other side!"

Grandma Ollie hugged Terri then held her at arm's length. "Girl, I see me in you in so many ways."

"Your eyes," Terri began an itemized list, "your temper."

"Well, don't act like I'm the originator. Don'tcha know? Family ways are passed down like hand-me-down clothes. From my mother I wear her red-boned skin, her fiery temper, and a love of hats. From my daddy, I wear his woolly hair and his fierce idea of right and wrong."

"I guess," Terri shrugged, "that's why I wanted to be a lawyer so bad: You passed that righteousness along to me."

Grandma Ollie nodded. "We both got it from him. It was that fierce sense of right and wrong that I ran into when I was packing my things to meet up with Hank back at Lovers Rock. Terri, girl, that was such a long spell ago, but when I close my eyes right here, I can see my daddy . . ."

Ollie's father wasn't a big man, but when he stood in the doorway that night he cast a shadow clear across the room, blocking the candlelight from the dresser and the moonlight through the window.

"Daddy," Ollie gasped, "you scared me."

"I didn't scare you 'cause I was quiet, I scared you because you know you doing wrong."

"I-I-I was gonna tell you, Daddy."

What's he thinking? Ollie wondered. What's he going to say? Gonna do?

"What's got a hold on you that'll make you run away from me in the middle of the night? That ain't like you. Look me in the eye, Ollie, 'cause we only got each other, and tell me what's wrong?"

And Ollie knew the right thing to do was to speak the truth; and the truth rolled off her tongue like a great cleanser, washing down the walls, scouring the floors, brightening the space between Ollie and her father. She told him everything. *Everything.*

"Never liked that jackleg joker, never did. Ollie baby," he said, "don't go."

Ollie drew back. "That's why I was hush. I knew you were going to say that. I've gotta grow up sometime."

"I know that better than you Ollie. I know you gotta grow up too. But this man is not for you. He's crooked. In his thoughts and in his ways, gambling . . . lying . . . stealing . . ."

"He had to, Daddy." Ollie threw a blouse into the open cardboard suitcase on her bed. "Mr. Forester was cheating Hank."

"And what else is new? You think Hank is the first? White men been cheating colored men since the beginning of time. That doesn't make what Hank did right—"

"He fought back, not like the rest of the men around here, dropping their eyes and acting like it's okay to take seconds."

"You only been 'round that boy since the sun went down and already you talking crooked too, Ollie." Her father stepped over by her side. "Fighting back wouldah been to quit and stop making Mr. Forester all that money and going to strike out on his own. Hank walks a crooked path, and if you go off and marry him, you gotta go that way too."

Ollie dropped her eyes.

"Can you trust a man that walks a crooked path? Can you keep loving a man that puts you on a crooked path too? What else will he lie about? I'm not advising you out of loneliness, Ollie, I'm just telling you how I see it. I could stop you if I really wanted to."

"No, you couldn't," Ollie said, shutting the suitcase.

Her father chuckled, turned, walked out onto the front porch, and sat in the swing. When Ollie walked to the door she saw him sitting there. She drew her body tall and marched out the door, stood not two feet away from her father so he could see her.

"You'll be back, Ollie Mae. You got too much of me in you to go . . ."

Terri stared at her grandmother who, without warning,

had fallen silent. She waited and waited for Grandma Ollie's next word. Terri felt loose like a faulty hinge, waiting to be straightened out. "C'mon, Grandma Ollie, c'mon."

With a quiver in her voice, Grandma Ollie answered softly . . .

"I walked and I walked. Every step I took made it harder for me to catch my breath. And the moon was wobbling all over the sky because I was glancing up at it through tears; and my tears made it magnify all big and loosey goosey. I kept thinking: I love him. I do. But this don't feel right. And what did I start thinking that for. Chile, I commenced to sweating, hard sweat all down my face and up under my bosom. Couldn't have been any wetter if I hadda fell into the river."

Instinctively Terri took her grandmother's hand. "You were stressed out and your body was tripping out on you."

"I'm not sure what it was; it was something else though. The ground started pitching up at me, Terri. I started walking crooked. I felt sick as a dog. By the time I reached Lovers Rock I must have been truly a sight, 'cause Hank grabbed me and had this crazy look in his eyes. And I just told him. 'I can't go. I can't. I love you but it's against all the nature in me.' What did I say that for? Hank hugged me so tight; I felt the skin rubbing against my rib cage like a hanky against a washboard. My tears wet his back and his tears wet mine."

"What did Hank say?"

"He pushed me away, started looking around on the ground. This way he looked and that way he looked. Finally Hank bent down and grabbed a handful of dirt with his right hand then his left."

Terri leaned in closer.

"I asked Hank, 'Whatcha doing?' Hank opened his right hand and there was the hair from my comb. He said, 'I got these wings that fell off an angel.' Then Hank took and opened his left hand and there were my toenail clippings. He said, 'I got these stars that fell out of the sky. I need something to remember you by. My girl don't love me no more.' "

Grandma Ollie's eyes got misty as she paused before beginning again.

"And Terri, chile, before I could say much of anything, Hank kissed me right softly, right quick before turning and running away. I couldn't move, Terri. I was rooted there. It was one of the worst days and one of the best days of my life."

Terri was confused. "How's that?"

"I had to let my first love go, but I realized that I had a powerful spirit that wouldn't let me do something so opposite of my nature, no matter how bad I wanted to. It's the spirit inside you, Terri, that rises up and tells you in a true crisis what's left and what's right. What's the straight path to take or what's the sleuth-footed way to go. And that's key. Baby, it's the small places and spaces in time that can alter your life forever. That was mine, I do believe. Lord, it was the worst of days. It was the best of days. And there'll be a day like that for you too. I see it. Sure as you born, Terri, I see it coming."

Chapter 17

It was Grandma Ollie who saw it coming, but it was Terri who read the signs.

She had inherited the gift from Grandma Ollie, who they said got it from her mother, the best friend of Mama Root. That's why Mama Root had tried so hard to get Grandma Ollie ready as a child, to show her how to use the gift of gut, as she liked to call it.

Terri was of the contemporary generation of women who'd come a long way baby but didn't particularly like to look back. So at times it bothered Terri, these strange, quirky but powerful instincts she experienced. They were gut feelings: a tingling here, a sensation there. In a few baffling incidences, it was knowing what was going to happen before it did—stuff that didn't jibe with logic or education.

Now, quiet as it's kept, a sign of budding romance is easy

to read. Terri's eyes began to sparkle. Lynnwood began giving the doorbell three staccato rings when he stopped by.

It was amazing how much joy could be found in a few short hours of the day. Lynnwood would come by after work looking sweet as he stood, glancing down, picking at a make-believe speck on the screen door before asking, "Wanna go for a walk?"

Terri was a millennium sister; up until now her exercise had centered on vigorous workouts at the Hyde Park Fitness Club. Every year a personal trainer banked a wallet load of Benjamins for taking Terri through the paces until her body was soaked with sweat.

Terri would battle with those fitness machines; but when it was over, she felt like she was losing the war. Her thighs and arms could still stand to be tighter. The scale read the same. So more often than not, Terri would feel a little frustrated the day after her workout.

But on long walks with Lynnwood, her body responded with vigor. She didn't feel tired. It seemed that the more they walked, the better she felt. Her blood pumped, her mind churned. They talked and shared simple things effortlessly; favorite colors, authors, and foods.

Lynnwood liked royal blue. Terri adored red, like Grandma Ollie. Lynnwood liked Chester Himes. Terri couldn't get enough of J. California Cooper. Lynnwood would walk a country mile on his hands for a good steak and a bowl of peach cobbler. Terri couldn't resist seafood gumbo and a bowl of banana pudding.

"But I can't have either of them nearly as much as I'd like."

Terri patted her hips with the flat of her hands. "The day after I'm so sluggish it takes me more than an hour to put a couple of miles on the treadmill."

Lynnwood responded simply, "A woman's body is built for comfort not for speed."

Then with a sweet deliberate momentum of his own, Lynnwood took Terri's hand and kissed it; then he walked her beneath a tree, and with his back up against the sturdy trunk, he pulled her close.

It was a passive-aggressive move; easy and slow enough for Terri to resist if she was of a mind to—and firm enough to trigger a sexual trembling in the pit of her stomach. This was the first time the two of them had walked past this tree.

It was a magnificent oak. If the brush and surrounding flowers were subjects, this tree would be their king. When the wind hailed its greatness, the crown of the tree responded with a courtly bow.

Physically Terri and Lynnwood were humble in the oak's presence; spiritually this was a bighearted moment for the both of them.

"So," Lynnwood said shyly, holding her hand against his chest. "Is there anything you want to ask me?"

"Mmmmm," Terri purred, thinking like the lawyer she was. "You should never ask a question unless you know the answer."

"That's up north."

"Oh really."

"In the South you can always ask a question, but you have to take the answer as gospel."

"That's some serious trust."

"Which every human being deserves until they prove otherwise. So when in Rome . . ."

"Okay, my question is: What did you think when you first met me?"

"I thought, Looks like this woman is single-handedly keeping Kleenex in business."

Terri shook her head in disbelief.

Lynnwood laughed and raised his free hand in an oath-taking position. "I swear."

"And what do you think of me now?"

"I think you're searching for romance the way the Pilgrims searched for a new world."

Terri turned quickly and dropped her chin.

Lynnwood raised it with his fingertips. "My question is: They did good. Why shouldn't you?"

Terri answered him with a kiss and Lynnwood took it as gospel.

The chapter and verse of things to come was faultless. Terri and Lynnwood were not members of the new-wave crowd. No, the *new-wave kicking it crowd* would have made the soft area beneath the tree their bed. They would have made the solitude a curtain to be drawn around them as their bodies had a fling. They would have added a bump and grind to the elements, upsetting the natural order of things.

Terri and Lynnwood were different. For that moment and space they found an innocent place, with room enough for two, that was even blessed with a view. They found no need to disturb the quiet; they became a part of all the pureness that was around them. Simply sitting together, holding each other tight. A genuine gift of appreciating that each could share this time with the other—no strings attached. No matter what happened in the days to come, they would have this simple, beautiful experience in common.

Every man and woman needs to be able to share chaste time together. And that Terri could do this with Lynnwood she read as a good sign.

The bad sign was less than forty-eight hours away.

Conflict began approaching as Friday grew near. No word from Zelda. Haji was monitoring the situation closely. She was a friend to every secretary and paralegal in the department. Haji had worked for the city so long, she'd planted the grapevine herself.

"There's some rumbling going on around here," she told Terri. "The associates on the case say they hear something funky is hanging it up. B and A isn't saying a peep, so they don't know what. Heard from Zelda? Is she budging?"

"From what I can tell, no."

"I don't like it. Do you know Annie, Morgan's secretary?"

"Yeah," Terri said, visualizing the woman.

"She says Morgan has been on edge all this week. She says something is bugging him but she doesn't know what."

Had Morgan gotten wind of the situation? If he had, why not call? Was he planning some kind of ambush? Morgan and Terri had a good relationship, but when it comes to work—anyone can be cut off at the knees, at any point in time.

Just as that thought percolated through Terri's mind, the call-waiting signal began to tap on the line.

"Haji, hold on." She clicked over. "This is Terri."

"Terri, this is Crenshaw."

Her stomach lurched.

"Crenshaw. Haven't spoken to you in a while. Please, let me get rid of this other call."

Then she grew calm. Fine, let's see what's what.

"Haji, that's Crenshaw. I've gotta—"

"What-he-say? What-he-say?"

"Nothing yet." Terri was getting calmer and calmer. "I'll keep you posted."

She started getting into lockdown mode. Take-a-blow, give-a-blow mode. Terri could take pressure better than a deep-sea diver. She clicked back over to Crenshaw.

"I hope this call is to tell me you're ready to settle."

His laugh was cold.

Terri pictured his rustic, tanned face, his thick eyebrows, bald head, and ice-cube-shaped glasses sitting on top of some nearby brief—he only used the glasses by hand to read, was too vain to put them on.

"Terri, thanks. That's the best laugh I've had all day. I haven't heard anything that funny since the Comedy Store."

"That's good to know. I knew I was a top lawyer, a good skier, even a great dancer. Now, thanks to you, I know I'm a comedian. *I don't think so.*"

"Terri, you're on guard fast. So it must be true."

"It's true that we have the upper hand on this case, and it's true that we're tired of playing litigation Ping-Pong with B and A. Yes, all that's true."

"Maybe it's true," Crenshaw overemphasized, "that you

sabotaged Zelda Jenkins because she wouldn't give you inside information about the case."

"Please, Crenshaw, that's the way you act, not me."

"Really? I believe you're up for a Golden Globe for this one. A couple of people caught your act—Zelda, your friend's secretary."

Terri paused. Crenshaw thought it was from fear, but it was a pause of deep thought. Grandma Ollie always said, *Chile, when somebody is trying to get your goat, let 'em have it and act like it's no big deal. Then see if they don't give it right back.*

"Listen, whatever went on between Zelda and me is between us, much the same as what goes on between you and the boys on the golf course. So if you want to make a stink over nothing and look silly in the eyes of your colleagues doing so, be my guest."

Crenshaw paused, expecting a war of words; he seemed surprised he didn't get one.

Leave it alone, Terri thought, leave it alone.

"Terri why don't we talk this over at the American Bar Association dinner tomorrow night? Come to the Hyatt early and let's have cocktails."

"I'm not going this year."

"That's unusual. You never miss it."

"I'm in Arkansas. My grandmother is ill."

"Oh, I'm sorry to hear that." Crenshaw's tone melted. "Terri, look. I think you're a heck of an attorney. Admired you at Sigmore and Barnes. Why not settle with us, throw us a million? That's a penny dropped in the street for a city like Chicago. Who'll know you backed off? Who'll care?"

Terri listened intently.

"This kind of deal happens more often than not, Terri. Don't you see? You're getting into the top echelon now. Morgan says he expects you to go far, maybe even into politics. And you don't want something like this hanging in your closet when the powers that be come courting. I'd sure hate to be the one who dirtied your dress."

"We're right and you're wrong, Crenshaw."

"Don't be naive, dear. It doesn't become you; clashes terribly with your smarts. So let me lay it on the line. If I don't hear from you by Monday morning, I'm going to go to Morgan. All my numbers are the same. You know where to find me?"

"Yeah," Terri said sweetly, "at work, home, or stuffing some poor lawyer in your back pocket."

Terri hung up the phone and the last thing she heard was a laugh from Crenshaw that put a chill in her bones.

Chapter 18

But bringing Grandma Ollie home from the hospital would warm Terri's soul.

"What's eatin' you?" Grandma Ollie asked as Terri kissed her on the cheek and sat in the chair by her hospital bed. Terri quickly changed the subject.

"Did they walk you today, Grandma?"

"Walked the stew out of me. Felt like Flo-Jo but didn't go nowhere but from this bed to the door and back."

Suddenly a distinct smell caught Terri's attention. She frowned at Grandma Ollie and raised an eyebrow. "Who's been sneaking food in here?"

Grandma Ollie rolled her eyes upward in a mischievous Bill Cosby fashion.

"Oh, I guess your lips are sealed."

"And satisfied too. Had me some deer."

"What? You're not supposed to be eating that old gamy meat."

"G'on 'way from here. That meat was good. And tender? Bet the butter, baby. My friend cooks it good—by her not having any teeth, it's falling off the bone."

"But you just had an operation, Grandma Ollie."

"On my hip. It ain't worth two cents. But my mouth is worth more than the U.S. mint. It works just fine."

Who could do anything with Grandma Ollie? Terri surrendered in thought before casting a long glance out the window.

Grandma Ollie studied her granddaughter. My child is not happy, she thought. "Terri, Lynnwood was by today and read to me for near 'bout two hours."

The hard line in Terri's jaw softened.

"I like that boy. He's sturdy, not a flimflammer like *some* young men I know."

Terri caught the signifying remark against Derek. She hadn't thought of him in a while. Was it because of the work drama that had trailed her here to Arkansas, or was it because of her developing relationship with Lynnwood?

Derek had left messages on her answering machine at home. She had Haji tell him she was out of town in New York on business.

When Terri *had* thought of Derek, it was at night. She would see a shadow bouncing against the window and recall his *smooth*. She'd hear a bird coo and recall some of his sweet nothings rolling around in her ear. She'd feel a trace of rain and recall how he handled her when they made love.

"Where are you?" Grandma Ollie asked, pulling Terri's attention back to her.

Terri just shrugged, Nowhere, then smiled.

"Humph, listen here. Did I ever tell you about the first big party I went to after Hank left?"

Terri shook her head no.

"Well sir, let me tell the story. You know I'd been heart-broken. Moped around, moped around. My daddy said he was tired of looking at me round that house, my bottom lip dragging the floor. He told me to get on to the church social that Saturday night. Said I was gonna go if'n he had to take me his self. Now, who wants to go to a dance with their father? Not a girl worth her pepper. Deep down inside, I believe I was ready to get out again."

"How long had it been since Hank left?"

" 'Bout three months. I had a great wallow going. I put on a pity dress every morning and walked around leading sorrow's parade."

"It was time to let that go."

"I mean, chile. Now Saturday morning Daddy went to do a job way over in the other county. He said I'd better go to that dance, though, 'cause he'd be by later on to check. I invited my best friend, Jilly, over."

"Miz Jilly!" Terri exclaimed. "I'd almost forgotten about her. She made the best candy apples, God rest her soul."

"Jilly could bake her butt off, Terri. When we were young women coming up, Jilly always said she'd get married first 'cause a man could always get a pretty face but a first-rate cook was hard to find. Jilly always had some boys hanging around the back of her house whenever she was baking."

"She baked that well, Grandma Ollie?"

"Chile, I heard one boy say, 'Her face is from hell but her cakes is from heaven!' "

"Oh, that's foul."

"I'm tellin' ya true, Terri. Now, this night Jilly was at my house, had already made a batch of cookies for the social. Had brung me a store-bought dress to wear that had gotten too small for her— sampling all them sweets had made *her tide rise to flood level* if ya know what I mean."

Terri laughed.

"Now, this was the prettiest dress I'd ever seen—it was sky blue with white lace around the short sleeves that bunched up around your upper arms. The material was fabulous, what you say! And full, lookah here, creases laid on your lap like the sheets on this bed. I mean! I put that dress on and felt good for the first time in months. I spied myself in the mirror and realized something was missing. Now, Terri, tell me, baby— what on earth could be missing?"

"A hat?"

"G'on with your bad self. That college degree you got ain't just a piece paper in a frame. That's right. We looked around at the hats I had but didn't nothing work. Terri, don't you ever—"

"I know: Go somewhere really special without a hat that matches your outfit. Go hatwearing or go home."

"Sho' ya right. Now you talking like my grandchild. Well, I wasn't about to go to that social without a hat. And I wasn't gonna *not* go 'cause I didn't want Daddy getting after me. So I looked around and looked around. And then something caught my eye. Know what?"

Terri shook her head no.

"We had a big old pretty lamp in the window of the front room. Sat by the window just like your Aladdin lamp does now at home."

Terri smiled.

"Only this lamp had a blue satin covering with a white lacy sash. My mother had bought it twenty years afore from a woman she used to serve parties for. Had to stand on her feet for five hours serving tea on Easter and still had to give the lady a dollar to boot, my daddy said. Made him mad. But Mama got the best of that deal, I swear. That lamp looked like something out of the movies. And I got good use of it too."

"How?"

"When me and Jilly figure out a plan, it's dangerous, Terri. Shoot, we bent the wiring in the shade and flattened it up against the inside braid, going all the way around. Then I put that bad boy on my head, tilted it back, and looked in the mirror: A star was born, what you say!"

"Nooooo," Terri hooted, slapping her hands together, then falling back in her chair. "Don't tell me that."

"The truth'll set you free, or at least get you out on parole."

"You went to the dance with a lamp shade on your head? And nobody but you and Miz Jilly knew?"

"I didn't say that."

Terri raised both hands to her mouth and giggled. "Who busted you out? One of your girlfriends?"

"Nope, your great-granddaddy."

"Awww, Grandma Ollie."

"Your grandmama was styling, like you young folks like to say. I was on the dance floor, getting spun here and there. Every time I turned around somebody was remarking how lovely I looked—especially about the head. One neighbor, can't recall who, said, 'Look how good that hat catches the light.' And who but my daddy piped up and said, 'That's 'cause it's made for light. Ollie Mae, why you got your ma's lamp shade on your head?' "

Grandma Ollie chuckled at the memory, then looked sheepishly at Terri. "It was good embarrassment. Folks laughed and I laughed with them. Even Daddy smiled. I felt human again. I'd been walking 'round emotionally dead over losing Hank. Remember, baby, it's okay to hurt but don't ever let anything or anybody make you numb inside. Get up from there and do something. Hear me? Arrange your own survival. Don't wait for somebody to come to the rescue, bring your own self back to life."

Chapter 19

But Terri wondered, Did her survival depend on her flying back to Chicago now?

"I know what you're thinking," Haji said at the start of their important telephone conversation. "You're thinking about coming home."

"Grandma Ollie is being released from the hospital to-morrow."

"That's kinda quick."

"You know how these hospitals are these days. They boot patients out as quick as possible."

"But how'll your grandmother get around?"

"They're sending a bed that we can set up off the kitchen so it'll be easier for her. Grandma Ollie doesn't really need me, Haji. I can pay to have someone come in. Plus Sugar was going to help anyway. Grandma Ollie doesn't really need me."

"Are you asking me or just trying to convince yourself, which is it?"

Terri sighed.

"Terri?"

"Make my flight arrangements for Sunday morning. I'll come home and crash—then go in blazing on Monday morning."

Haji was silent for a few seconds. "I'm not trying to get in your business—"

"Then don't." Terri was truly sorry for how that sounded. She quickly added, "Please."

"Okay. I'll make the arrangements. Anything else you need?"

Terri didn't need anybody else throwing a chip of doubt in the kitty. That's why she had so quickly silenced Haji. Her conscience was already calling the bluff. But what choice did she have?

To stay would jeopardize all that Terri had worked for. Her career and her reputation were on the line. Hard knock by hard knock Terri had taken some of the worst blows while struggling along the path of a professional black woman. But this—this could be a knockout punch. Terri felt she had to slip it.

The hardest part would be telling both Grandma Ollie and Lynnwood.

For him, it would have to be this evening: the sooner the better. It wasn't like she was going to disappear from the face of the earth and never come back. So what was she so keyed up about? The answer was significant. It was because of something Grandma Ollie had said.

Baby, it's the small places and spaces in time that can alter your life forever.

Grandma Ollie could get deep on you like that. You could be watching the soaps on TV, chilling out with some chips and dip. And in between the chip breaking off in the dip and you fishing it out during the commercial, Grandma Ollie would drop something deep on you; throw something on your mind. She could be a signifying diva or a southern Socrates. Either way it would make your mouth drop open.

Baby, it's the small places and spaces in time that can alter your life forever.

Terri would have to deal with Lynnwood first; he promised to be by the house this evening and sounded very excited about it, more so than usual.

Terri knew what she wanted to say. The how of it all would be direct; the where of it all was a complete surprise.

"No Lovers Rock today. Let's walk the other way. I have a surprise."

He sounded like a kid and was throwing off an energetic aroma like other men throw off cologne. That made Terri's body perk up. Her mind said, Tell him now. Tell him now. Her heart said, What's the surprise?

Lynnwood and Terri walked to a building that had once been a small plane hangar. Terri remembered it from her childhood—this plain wooden structure that had been a hangar during World War II. Over in the next county was an air force base. During the big war, damaged planes were stored at this hangar in Collingswood; they would bring a bad one there and strip it for parts. The place was only big enough to hold one plane at a time. Not very practical. After the war, the military lost interest in the gangly structure that was already out of date even before the dedication ribbon was cut.

The colored folks of Collingswood used to have barn dances inside the hangar up until 1979, when so many of the young folks started going away to school and not coming back. Some of the old-timers around town kept the place up with their own money; keeping the whitewash clean, oiling the door hinges. But pretty much the place hadn't been used since the early 1990s.

Lynnwood opened the door of the hangar. The light from outside streamed in through slits in the ceiling spaces like rainbows peaking through clouds in the sky. The glowing speckled yellow light bebopped around them. Terri felt incredibly warm. She stood on packed dirt so smooth it actually resembled a hardwood floor. The walls were clean; whitewash complimenting the wide, open space.

"Ain't it great? I loved this old place since I was a kid. We're gonna decorate it up for the big dance."

"The Summer Social?" Terri asked. "Three months away?"

He nodded.

"That's a lot of work."

"Me and the guys from church, some of the old vets, we're gonna swing it. Got that big Home Depot out near the old air force base to donate the goods. They said it would be good publicity."

"Wow, that was cool."

"Well, I can't take all the credit. I've been hanging around a lawyer. My power of persuasion has improved a whole lot."

Lynnwood winked. He moved closer to Terri. "I think we've really been good for each other."

Terri's heart lurched: one, because it was true, and two, because she knew she had to tell him.

"Imagine," Lynnwood said, circling his hand around Terri's waist. "Our grandparents danced here."

Lynnwood pulled her close. His head dropped low on her shoulder, his back bending. He began a slow rocking dance back and forth.

"My grandfather loved this place. My daddy too. He was a rodeo man like me. Runs in the family. And you know what? My grandfather asked my grandmother to renew their wedding vows right here at the Summer Social of '79."

Terri felt his body, firm and strong against hers. They moved slowly to the left, slowly to the right.

"I was out back lighting firecrackers with my friends. Between all that popping, we noticed the music had stopped and we heard everybody go, 'Aaaaaahh.' We ran inside and there were Granddaddy and Grandmamma in the center of the room dancing by themselves. He was singing to her. Could barely hear it."

"How sweet is that . . ."

"I come from a long line of sweet men, girl. I wish I could remember what the song was. Let me see here, went a little something like this . . ."

Terri's face flushed crimson as Lynnwood began humming in her ear.

And the song was not familiar to either of them. It came from within; it was in their fingertips that clutched each other's back. It was in the bottoms of their feet gliding across the dirt floor. It was on their lips, parting gently for the sound of romance that was escaping from their souls.

And with them holding each other close like that, Terri could feel her own heart beating. Lynnwood inhaled her cologne and at that moment valued it more than air. He broke their embrace for just a moment to spin Terri. And in that sliver of space and seconds, Terri found both voice and courage, but of neither of them was she proud.

"I have to go, Lynnwood."

He kept turning her. "We just got here."

Physically Terri's body spun slowly; mentally her mind was spinning out of control.

"No, I'm going home to Chicago."

Lynnwood let go. And the music they had together stopped like a needle screeching across an old 45 record.

"You're leaving?" He looked at her across the space that seemed to expand with each breath they took. "Why?"

"I've got a big problem at work . . ."

A sound similar to an air brake releasing leapt from Lynnwood's lips. "Forget work."

"I can't forget it, Lynnwood, it's important."

"You just got here. Grandma Ollie is coming home. Who's going to take care of her?"

"I'm paying someone to come in, and Sugar will help. I've got a problem that I have to deal with back in Chicago. I'll be back . . ."

"When? You'll get so busy. You'll forget about everybody, including me."

The guilt that rushed up from Terri's gut got stuck in her throat. She turned away, and when her eyes lost sight of Lynnwood, she was able to say, "I don't need this right now."

Lynnwood turned her around. "Then stay. Take care of your grandma and let what we have grow. Don't be silly and selfish."

"Silly and selfish?"

"Yeah. You're worrying about a career. That's so silly. I mean, dog, it's just a thing. Think about people, Terri."

"That quote unquote 'thing' was a dream that Grandma Ollie and I shared together. It was a seed she planted, telling me as a little girl that I could be somebody. When I told her I was going to graduate first in my high school class, she said why not college too? When I said I wanted to be a lawyer, she said why not a judge? Every dream doesn't come out of thin air; some dreams others plant inside your head to share. So please don't simplify my situation with your backwards Mayberry attitude."

Lynnwood started backing away. "Excuse me, miss. I must be on the wrong side of the map. Let me take my country ass on."

"Wait a minute . . ."

Lynnwood kept backing away.

"I once said I'd walk a country mile to be round a pretty woman. Looks like I'm about to walk a country mile to get away from one."

"Wait . . ."

But Lynnwood walked away and Terri walked home alone. Sadness and solitude threw a party inside her head, and the things Terri was worried about started dancing around in her mind.

Work and romance were doing the bump.

Insecurity was moonwalking.

The party lasted all night long. Just like people, sometimes our problems just don't know when to go home. Terri awoke with a dilemma hangover. But it would be the hair of the dog that bit her that would save Terri.

Chapter 20

"Terri, your feet must be hurting, you've been running through my mind all day long."

Grandma Ollie was sitting up in the chair, clothed in a beautiful teal-blue dress. "Did you find 'em?"

Terri nodded. She had spent much of the morning driving around with Sugar looking for teal house shoes. Grandma Ollie couldn't wear her dress shoes and refused to leave the hospital unless her feet were matching the rest of the outfit.

"Found them," Terri said, taking the shoes out of the box, kneeling to slip them on her feet.

Grandma Ollie gently touched her head. "I'm so glad you're here with me. It means a lot to this old woman."

Terri nearly gagged on thin air. Almost two days had passed, and she still had not summed up the pepper to tell Grandma Ollie she was leaving.

"Get my hat, my gloves, and my bag."

Terri got them from the closet, all the things she had bought before as ordered. "You know you're leaving the hospital, not giving a fashion show."

"G'on 'way from here, chile. Let's roll."

A nurse brought in a wheelchair. Terri held the wheelchair as Grandma Ollie made the two or three steps to get into it. "Very good, Grandma."

She grinned from ear to ear. "Let's blow this pop stand, kid."

Terri began to wheel Grandma Ollie down the hall. The nurses began to remark, "Bye, Miss Ollie! Don't she look good, y'all?"

Grandma Ollie smiled and waved like she was in a parade. "Drive slow, Terri," she fussed. "Folks is admiring. Give 'em ample time."

Terri slowed down to a snail's pace. Grandma Ollie said all her good-byes and they made it home with no trouble. Cousin Sugar and her son, Cube, were already there along with Deacon Homer.

"Welcome home!" Sugar said, meeting the car in the carport. Cube was tagging along behind his mother as usual.

"Sister Ollie," Deacon Homer said, kissing her on the cheek. He helped her out of the car and into the wheelchair that the hospital had delivered the day before. "I stopped by to drop off a card. Terri told me she was gonna fetch you right home so I just had to wait."

"They're putting you on the sick and shut-in list in the church bulletin." Terri updated Grandma Ollie as they all made their way back toward the house.

Deacon Homer was grinning. "Don't know why. Pretty as you are, Miss Ollie, you sure don't look like no sick person."

"Say I don't!"

"No, you look as good as these two young gals you got here with you. Look like you're thirty-something too."

"Awww, c'mon." Cube laughed and began running ahead.

Grandma Ollie stuck her cane out and tripped Cube up but good. Softly, he went tumbling down rolling on the grass. Everyone looked at Grandma Ollie, stunned. She dropped her eyes sheepishly. "Lord, forgive me."

They all laughed.

Once inside Grandma Ollie insisted on sitting up to talk to her company for a while. "Did you go to Brother Robinson's funeral?"

"Yes indeed. And let me say to glory, that young girl put him away fine. Mighty fine."

"Humph." Grandma Ollie cut her eyes low then turned up the corner of her mouth. "Amazin' she had some money left. That wife of his spent money like it was going out of style. That girl was half his age. That's probably what killed him, trying to satisfy her."

Deacon Homer grinned. "Don't know if that caused his death, but it did cause some problems for the funeral director. They had to have a closed casket."

"He died of natural causes. Why the closed casket?"

"Said Brother Robinson had taken so much Viagra he remained at attention even after embalming; so they didn't dare leave it open—and say they could barely close the top."

Grandma Ollie caught the twinkle in Deacon Homer's eye

and they both began to laugh. "You can sho' kid like the devil sometimes, Deacon Homer. Lookah here, where's the card you brought me?"

"Here," Sugar said, taking it off the table. "Want me to open it for you?"

"No," Grandma Ollie said, whisking it out of her hand. She whispered to Terri, "Might be some money in it."

Grandma Ollie opened the card and made a demonstrative shake of it to show that there wasn't a single cent in it. She glanced at the cover and smiled sweetly. "Isn't this nice?"

"Naw," Cube piped up, "he supposed to put some money in it." Sugar grabbed a dishrag and snapped his arm. "Awwww! That hurt."

"Leave that baby alone," Miss Ollie ordered, cutting her eyes at Deacon Homer. "And a little child shall lead them."

He cleared his throat. "Uh . . . uh, well." Then changed the subject. "How did you enjoy your stay at the hospital?"

"I'm glad to be home. But the people there, all of them are real nice."

"Ain't that the truth. Remember, Miss Ollie, I was in there last year for prostate surgery."

"What's a prostate?" Cube asked, then jumped before his mother could load up the dishrag.

"Let's just say prostate is another name for penis," Deacon Homer attempted to explain.

Cube frowned. "Why does it have two names?"

" 'Cause it's important!" Deacon Homer answered with extra bass in his voice.

Terri, Sugar, and Grandma Ollie got tickled. They tried to

conceal it but that was like holding your breath underwater. Their jaws began to swell. Their eyes bugged. The three women looked to one another for rescue. They might as well have tossed one another an anchor to hold on to because that exchange of glances only sank their gallant attempt at restraint. Basically, it was on.

The giggle started with Terri. Small, dainty, stuffed down, trying not to be rude. Sugar let loose with two strong snorts, like a bull tearing out of a rodeo stall. And Grandma Ollie? She felt she was too old to be trying to keep from laughing at Deacon Homer, might cause a heart attack or worse—the passing of gas. Grandma Ollie threw her head back and let it fly. She laughed so hard her poly couldn't get a grip—and her dentures slipped forward and fell right into her lap.

"Oops! Help me, Jesus," she gummed.

When Terri saw that, her hands flew to her mouth, smothering the laughter heaving up from her gut. Now Deacon Homer and Cube were laughing too. Sugar was flat-out crying. The picture of a bowl of fruit hanging on the kitchen wall fell.

"Lord," Grandma Ollie said, still laughing, "that's a bad sign."

"It's a sign y'all women are crazy up in here," Deacon Homer was forced to testify.

The doorbell rang.

Sugar dabbed at her eyes with the dishrag. "Get that, cuz. That's Lynnwood I'm sure. Time for y'all to make up."

Terri stumbled over to the front of the house, holding her side, still laughing. I'll tell him I'm sorry too, she thought. I won't forget him. How can I?

Terri opened the door and Derek was standing there.

Kamikazed by his eyes, by the curves of his mouth, by the way his jeans hugged his thighs, Terri fought to keep her heart from raising a white flag that would surrender her soul.

What is it about this man? That's what Terri asked herself. What is it?

Her heart answered for her. Derek had that thing happening. That thing that maybe one other person has in the universe that makes you unable to resist them. One person's frog is another person's prince. Derek had croaked for many women; but for his lady Terri he hoped to wear a crown.

That thing, that thing.

"I'm glad to see you laughing," Derek said. "That's a wonderful sign. You know how you and your grandmother like to read signs. Because you were smiling when the door opened, that's a sign there's hope for us."

Terri blushed, said nothing, but thought, Is it?

"Who's that?" Sugar said, coming over to the door. She saw Derek and jutted her neck. "Well, well, looky here."

"Can I come in? I'm in the South. Where's the hospitality?"

"We pamper our guests," Sugar said with a peachy smile, "but we shoot coons."

Derek laughed. "Sugar, you've still got that sweet smile and that bitter tongue."

Sugar leaned over and posed like an umpire. "I call 'em like I see 'em."

"Cool it, Sugar," Terri said, stepping aside. "Come on in, Derek."

As he walked through the door, Derek had his hands behind

his back. He whipped around two bouquets of roses; half a dozen in each—red, yellow, and pink mixed.

Terri was a sucker for roses. She felt her heart jump; on the three-month anniversary of their first date, Derek had given her a big bouquet of red, yellow, and pink roses.

Derek leaned forward, then spun, and handed one of the bouquets to Sugar.

"Hey now!" she said. "I like this."

Derek winked at Terri then sidestepped her, going straight to the living room.

Grandma Ollie guffawed. "Well, sir. Look what the wind blew in."

Derek handed her the bouquet. "Pretty flowers for a pretty lady."

Deacon Homer scratched his head. "You must own a flower shop the way you handing out roses, young man."

"No sir. Just a hardworking guy trying to show some love to the ladies that'll be part of my family soon."

Grandma Ollie and Sugar cut their eyes at Terri.

"Well, let me get on up from here," Deacon Homer excused himself. "Y'all got a lot to talk about I'm sure. Another time, Miss Ollie."

"Thanks for stopping by. Come anytime. You know my door always swings on welcome hinges."

The door shutting sounded like a gunshot; the room had become just that quiet. Derek let his glance fall from one woman to another.

More quiet.

Grandma Ollie finally spoke up. "You could hear an ant

piss on cotton in here. Sugar, roll me to the kitchen so we can put our flowers in some water. Cube, run on outside and play. These two have some talking to do."

As Sugar began to push Grandma Ollie past Derek, he reached out and touched her arm. "I've been wrong, Grandma Ollie. But I'm here now. And I'm going to be right."

Grandma Ollie patted his hand gently. "A leopard can't change his spots, Derek." She glanced up at Sugar. "Roll on, baby."

Seconds later it was only Derek and Terri in the room. For the first time since they met years ago, when they found each other's lips after accidentally being jostled together in a crowd, there was marked awkwardness between them.

Awkwardness is like a ghost: The presence is heartfelt and fleeting. Scary and intimidating, awkwardness instantly began to haunt their past relationship. Terri began to think of the things that had drawn her to Derek in the first place. His smooth. His smarts. His sex appeal. That's what had her hog-tied, Derek's sex appeal.

"Terri, I came here to tell you how sorry I am about what's gone on between us. I want to make it right."

"How'd you find out that I was here?"

"A little birdie told me."

"More like a jaybird named Haji no doubt."

"No, she didn't." Derek smiled mischievously. "Have you checked in with her lately? You should."

"When I do," Terri said sarcastically, "I'll let her know you arrived safely."

"It wasn't Haji. You forget I have ways of finding things out and getting things done. I'm a man of action."

"A little too much sometimes," Terri said blandly. "Look, I don't care how you found out I was here. All I know is that I've got a lot on my mind and you coming here right now isn't something I'm ready for."

"If I had called ahead of time and asked could I come, would you have let me?"

"I—"

"I nothing," Derek said, stepping forward and lifting her chin, closing her mouth with the tips of his fingers. "You wouldn't. You haven't returned my calls. You didn't even want me to know where you really were. You're a woman who likes to fry her judgment on a cast iron skillet. You didn't want to see me; you're afraid."

"Afraid of what?"

"Afraid of coming back to me, that's what. I don't deserve it. There. I punked out and said it. Told the truth. I don't deserve you back, but I want you back just the same. I'll do anything."

"Derek, I just need more time to think—"

"Show me the mountain and I'll climb it."

"I don't want to talk about this now. Sugar and Grandma Ollie are in the other room—"

"Go ahead and talk!" Grandma Ollie shouted from the kitchen. "We ain't listening to y'all."

"Sho not," Sugar yelled.

Terri looked at Derek and rolled her eyes. "See?"

"Come to my hotel later tonight. I rented a car. I'm at the

Comfort Inn on Route Three, just ten minutes away from here."

"If I'm not ready to talk, I'm certainly not ready to spend the night at your hotel room."

Derek held up both hands like someone had said, Stick 'em up. "Honest, baby, no hanky-panky."

Derek vanquished the space between them and whispered in Terri's ear, "It'll be a gut-check talk between you and me. And if it goes well, like I pray, we can enjoy some time here in Collingswood, maybe even fly back together."

Terri turned him toward the door. "No plans. No promises."

Derek began walking. "And I'll be waiting." He stopped just as Terri turned the doorknob. "Oh, I forgot your flowers." Then Derek reached into his suit pocket and pulled out a slender, black velvet box. He handed it to Terri.

Slowly her hand left the knob and she took it. "You can't buy me, Derek."

"Terri, a woman as fine as you is priceless. I'm not trying to buy you; I'm trying to please you."

Terri opened the box. Inside was a silver bracelet with little roses engraved on it. At the center were three small stones—red, white, and yellow—just like the flowers he had brought Grandma Ollie and Sugar.

When Terri looked up to tell Derek how pretty it was, he ducked his head and kissed her. "Tonight."

Then he vanished.

Grandma Ollie rolled into the living room. "Beware of Negroes bringing gifts. That boy could sell an Eskimo an icebox."

"So you want me to quit Derek and give back this bracelet and my engagement ring too?"

"Are you nuts? You don't ever give back a stitch of jewelry. Girl, I'll use your birth certificate for firewood. Quit him if you wanna, but keep the medals."

"Right, cuz," Sugar said to Terri before turning to Grandma Ollie. "Do you believe she's some kin to us?"

"I don't know. We better have the police run a DNA test!" Grandma Ollie grinned then cut her eyes at Terri.

Terri tried to force a smile but her insides were knotted up. Grandma Ollie patted Terri's hand. "Rest your brain for a while. Come help an old lady get comfortable."

Chapter 21

Sometimes getting comfortable isn't slipping into soft pajamas or having a glass of your favorite wine. Sometimes comfortable is the company you keep. Sugar and Cube went home and left Grandma Ollie and Terri to themselves.

In sanctified churches true believers are said to be able to speak in tongues. True believers of family are able to speak with their bodies. It's simple but real. It was the way Terri and Grandma Ollie changed the sheets on her bed: the old woman sitting in her wheelchair on one side and Terri on another. Each knowing when the other wanted to snap the bed's fragile skin before letting it fill with air, float down, and be tucked in on the sides.

It was the way Grandma Ollie cleared her throat and Terri went for herbal tea without being asked, one spoon of honey and two wedges of lemon. It was the way Grandma Ollie bent her back and curled her spine when Terri helped her onto the medical prop in the bathtub so she wouldn't have to strain her hip. Terri immediately got the soap and foamed her back, rubbing and massaging, each fold of skin, each wrinkle a line in the tedious story of how the body ages despite care.

The tingly feeling of the water against Terri's hands and the warmth of her grandmother's back; the motion of the constant rubbing soothed Terri. Grandma Ollie's muscles responded by relaxing, and that brought Terri immense joy, knowing that she was really pleasing this woman who once saved her from drowning in the womb.

The spiritual connection between the two women of the same blood, of the same hopes, of the same dreams became physical, pulsing at the tips of Terri's fingers and in the old woman's spine.

With just the sound of the water washing down Grandma Ollie's back and the soapy towel swabbing her arms, Terri felt a swelling inside her soul. She started to hum. It was heavy like the echo of the sloshing, soapy water, but full as a gospel refrain.

Terri began to rinse and hum, cupping her hands and raising them high before emptying them out. Her humming became deeper, resonating inside the room, penetrating both her and Grandma Ollie's skin. Before Terri realized it, the front of her own clothes was soaked and Grandma Ollie's back glistened like sunshine. She stopped humming and reached for a towel.

"Go on. Go on, baby girl, and sing out," Grandma Ollie whispered, "but where in heaven did you get that song?"

Any answer Terri gave would be true. She got the song from her soul. It had been hiding like lightning hides behind storm clouds in the sky. Could have gotten the song from there.

She got the song from wishes yet to be fulfilled. It had been hiding in the recesses of her conscience, waiting to bloom like seeds of spring. Could have gotten the song from there.

So instead of giving any answer that would be true, Terri gave an answer that was the most honest. "Grandma Ollie, I'm really not sure."

"You know," she laughed as Terri began to towel her off, "what I know as an experienced woman will put a young gal like you to shame. So instead of shaming you, I'm gonna share with you."

"Please, please," Terri begged.

"What I see is this: You sure of yourself one minute and insecure the next. I know that not having your mother and father to grow up with has left question marks in your heart about what a core family should be."

"I appreciate all you've done for me—"

"Don't doubt it. And I feel it. I feel that you do, baby. I'm not taking away from the glory that we have for each other. Can't nothing or nobody cast a shadow on that. No ma'am. Nobody need to even begin to try."

Terri helped her slip on her robe as they continued to talk and headed into the kitchen for tea.

"You have instincts, Terri, that you have to trust. When your gut tells you to do something, go on and do it. When you see a sign, follow it. Don't be afraid. Why do you have so much fear?"

"I just don't want to make a mistake, Grandma Ollie."

"A mistake? No matter what you do, baby, know this. You will never be a trailblazer when it comes to making a mistake. Many a woman has done that long before you, including Eve in the garden. A mistake ain't no big thang."

"Then I should go hear what Derek has to say?"

"You should do what you wanna do, not what I might advise you to do."

"I need to think about it."

"Then that's the path you take, Terri. Don't let Mr. Big Stuff come flying in here changing your time clock. This ain't daylight saving time. This is Terri saving time."

Terri kissed her grandmother's hand and helped put her to bed, covering her in a beautiful family quilt made shortly after slavery.

"Always remember," Grandma Ollie's voice cut through the darkness, "let your mind go blank and what you should do will be clear. And always remember this too: A woman listens to a man with her heart and not just her ears."

And with those words filling her soul, Terri went and sat quietly by herself, sipping the last of the tea. She let her mind go blank. *A clean slate will draw a clean decision.* She sat, the moon her company, its rays her light.

When her cell phone rang, she hesitated before answering it. Knowing it was late, she knew it surely had to be important.

"Hello?"

"Terri, this is Haji. How did you like your surprise?" She sounded joyous and excited.

"Derek showing up on my doorstep will not land a spot in my top ten favorites."

"What? He never said he was going down there. I thought he was going to call you on your cell."

"It's fine, Haji. I'm not mad at you for telling him where I was."

"I didn't. He called me about the B and A case. Didn't Derek tell you?"

"Tell me what? He said I should call you but I didn't think anything of it."

"Terri, that's the surprise. Zelda is dropping all the allegations against you. Crenshaw's leverage is out with the trash—and he can't blackmail you into settling. So you can stay there. And it's all thanks to Derek."

"What?"

"Derek told me that he and Crenshaw worked together before. He ran into him at the ABA dinner. Crenshaw was throwing back the bourbon and got a case of the loose lips. Derek overheard him talking about the B and A case and how he had you over a barrel and why."

"What a jerk."

"Okay? Anyway, Derek used to work with Crenshaw. He said he used to save the man's butt left and right. Crenshaw owed him. So Derek convinced Crenshaw to get Zelda to back off."

"Derek did that for me?"

"Sure did. Got it done. Derek called me this morning and

said everything was cool. I asked him how he pulled it off, and Derek said with an Uzi. Guess it pays to know where a body is buried."

"That's great," Terri said, a wave of relief rushing over her.

"But I swear, Terri, I didn't tell him you were at your grandma's—"

"I believe you." Terri thought back to her conversation with Crenshaw. "Crenshaw knew where I was. He had to be the one who told Derek."

"He must have flown down there after our conversation. Derek saved the day, Terri. He really did."

Terri knew that, knew it in her soul, and she nodded in the moonlight. "Derek is waiting for me now at the hotel. He's here in Collingswood, hoping we can save our relationship."

That's when the thought went crashing through Terri's mind: But what about Lynnwood?

What Terri didn't know about Lynnwood was that he was a doer. She knew he was a rodeo man who loved horses and liked to ride. That Terri knew. He was tough. Terri cringed while watching home videos of Lynnwood in a Georgia rodeo contest as the bronco jerked and snorted, throwing him to the ground, dragging him on his hindquarters more than ten feet just after he'd logged in the winning time.

Lynnwood's face was caked with dust; only his pearly grin was evident as he jumped up like *he had dragged the horse* instead of the other way around. The prize money he split with a friend. The man had gotten hurt two years before and wasn't able to work anymore.

That was Lynnwood's way.

It was also his way to be a leader, but this night, time and circumstance turned him into a follower. Lynnwood was driving up to Grandma Ollie's house. As he got into the truck, he had been embarrassed to be taking a road trip in hopes of rescuing his chances for true romance with Terri. Their romance resembled a bud not quite fully open, but nearly bursting with promise. It was the kind of thing that made you pray for its future because its potential was so overwhelming you knew only God could handle the request.

Lynnwood wasn't sure what he was going to say to Terri, but he knew she was leaving. When? Lynnwood had been so hurt that he couldn't remember exactly. Maybe it was tomorrow, Saturday? Whenever, he just couldn't let Terri go without pouring his heart out to her. Now, exactly what those words would be, he didn't rightly know. But Lynnwood wouldn't be able to live with himself unless he got in his truck and drove over to Miss Ollie's house to see Terri.

Lynnwood was pondering what to say as he turned the corner in the road near the house. His next sight gave him sore eyes. There was Terri walking to a car with some man.

How did Lynnwood know it was Derek? Instinct? Maybe. Or just a bad gut omen? Maybe.

Terri got in Derek's car and Lynnwood trailed at a distance with his lights off. He followed them until they reached the highway and traveled to a nearby hotel.

Lynnwood watched as Terri got out of the car and walked inside with Derek. He watched as Derek patted her back, and lightly turned her by the elbows with his fingertips.

The cache of comfort that this man had with Terri made

Lynnwood develop a taste of fear. He licked his lips nervously as he sat in the truck; the running motor jostled his body, and a trickle of sweat slowly meandered down the back of his tense neck.

"He ain't no fool," Lynnwood said out loud to himself. "He sure came after her."

Lynnwood made a wish. What did Lynnwood wish right at that moment? He wished that the moon would be on his side and cast a light across Terri's face. That light would be pure and natural and illuminate every nook of possibility and every cranny of hope.

What Lynnwood needed to see was Terri's romantic resolve. Was she hopelessly in love with Derek? Was there a chance? A rodeo man like Lynnwood knew: All a winner needs is a moment in time, a sliver of chance, and a heart of courage.

He hoped the hope. Lynnwood hoped in that stuffy air sweltering inside his truck, which didn't cost much, didn't look like much, but cranked up every time and still made it to the mark and back. Lynnwood clutched the steering wheel with his hands, his knuckles bulging. He was like the truck: His net worth wasn't much, he didn't turn many heads, but he rose to the occasion and met the mark every time.

Lynnwood glanced up at the sky. The stars were a posse of brilliance that roamed the open range of night. The moon steadied everything—the sky, time, and Lynnwood's rampaging heart.

Does Terri still love Derek? he wondered.

Whose side would the moon be on? Love or loss? Lynnwood needed to see Terri's face. He wasn't a miserable half man like some, too weak to fight for the woman he wanted or mistreating one that he really didn't.

Lynnwood was cut from a masculine cloth and stitched together with righteous seams. He had the guts to go after Terri but wouldn't if it wasn't going to be the best thing for her. Lynnwood wanted to see Terri happy. In the short time that they had known each other, he felt that. The hope for her joy was just as keen as his desire for Terri.

Lynnwood loved her smell the way a florist loves the scent of flowers. He sought her presence the way buds seek the sun. He felt they belonged together like black-eyed peas and rice. But did Terri know that?

Tonight the moon was on Lynnwood's side. As Terri and Derek stepped into the doorway of the hotel, she turned. And the moonlight blazed across her face. And in that flicker of shining, in that blink of space, Lynnwood saw doubt on Terri's face.

He pounded the steering wheel with both hands, drumming out a battle cry. He even yelped, and liked the way the sound bounced around his trusty vehicle and rolled to a whisper inside his own head. Opportunity was joy. Lynnwood saw a chance to win Terri's love. All he had to do now was find a way.

Chapter 22

Lynnwood was searching for a way while Terri and Derek were searching for a means. A means to an end, that is: That's what the powwow in the tiny Collingswood hotel room was. For Derek it meant finding voice to apologize for the doggish dirt that he had committed. His hope was to put it to rest by taking a bite out of Terri's nemesis Crenshaw and burying her problem like an unwanted, dried-out bone.

For Terri it meant finding herself, her emotional self and its bottom line. And at that bottom would be the top of the threshold that measured how strong Terri's love was for Derek—and furthermore what she would or would not take.

The words he chose were simple and promising, like seeds in the middle of a sliced apple. He planted them in her mind with lips pressed close to her ear as they sat next to each other on the bed.

Each sorry was of a different shape, of a different sound. Sad one minute, pitifully hip the next. Terri examined them in her mind—picked at them like a kid picks at unwanted veggies on a plate.

Grandma Ollie had told Terri, *A woman listens to a man with her heart and not just her ears.*

But when things got *funky monkey* like they were now between Terri and Derek, a girl damn near needed a hearing aid to make sense of what was going on.

Words have power but emotions are atomic. Terri listened and ached inside. She felt this thing for Derek and was having a tough time separating reason from magnetism.

And not just the physical; it wasn't just a jumping bones kind of a thing. A part of Terri felt she belonged with Derek, but reason, which can sometimes be the split personality of wanting, told her their relationship was as shaky as a LEGO set in a windstorm.

So it wasn't so much an acceptance of the sorrys but a submission of the flesh when Terri let Derek close after he whispered these words:

"Can I just be with you?"

So simple, so direct.

Derek kissed her in a place where he could feel her heartbeat against his lips. Moist and soft, tender and inviting, his lips tingled against her flesh.

Terri felt her heartbeat jump like a wounded animal, then settle back down rapid and cautious.

Derek prowled higher, kissing Terri on the breastbone. The room was so small it closed in on them like a muscle contracting, capturing them in a cocoon of skin, pulse, skepticism, and hope.

Where's this going? Terri began questioning herself relentlessly. Is this a mistake? Can I enjoy one thing without passing judgment on the other? Can I get down without giving in? If I do, is that selfish? And if it is, so what? Two can play that game. But do I wanna?

Terri looked into Derek's eyes and saw stars. Their fingers webbed together and their lips meshed. Derek and Terri's desire for each other was naked, and soon they were too. Just holding each other was like an injection of heat for the couple.

Derek said, in a scratchy, little boy's voice, "Let's remember when."

So a flashback of ancient labors of love filled their minds. Their bodies would wind together like thread around a spool; that spool being raw lust. Their lips would cascade down each other's body, a free and frisky waterfall.

They recalled their tender giggles. At the time they were learning each other's pleasure points. It was like finding needles in a haystack. But once found, the needles were used to burst their inhibitions.

The memories they shared now were not cheap thrills. They were genuine moments of exhilaration that, depending on decisions to come, would be part of their future history together from that point on, or their ancient history.

Caressing or tickling—the familiar things that couples do after comfort comes calling and is eagerly accepted by both man and woman.

Every touch remembered was not of the sensual kind; some were of the saving variety—saving as in the world is a bad mama-jamma and could you save me from it? Can I find a safe place to be in your shadow? Save a spot for me in your heart because a heartless world has beaten me down today.

Derek and Terri had swapped times like those, but surely not enough or this pain-in-the-butt dilemma would be curbed with the rest of the garbage that belonged to the world.

So they recalled the best of their physical times, trying to get in touch with their sensual connection. Had it been broken by betrayal or severed completely?

Derek said softly, "Terri, remember the sauna?"

In their history of having each other, the more comfortable they grew with each other, the more inventive they had become. Derek and Terri made love in a sauna that he managed to rent exclusively for two hours. The hot steam and the shortness of breath that a romp produces made it seem as if Terri was smothering. She felt the fullness of Derek's body and that of her own, expanding with each touch of their bodies—their tongues, their hips. Speaking of hips, their hips against the wooden slats seemed to simmer with the moisture from the steam and their stark desire.

Terri had been reserved at first, not that keen on the idea, but submissive. She was at that critical stage of a romance where she wanted to do things to continue to please Derek. Who knew that she would have so much fun herself?

Terri had fancied the steam to be a hot spring, bubbling from their pores. She felt regal as she stood looking down at Derek, a love servant, she imagined, who was emotionally shackled and ready to do whatever she asked. Terri had tied her towel around her waist, all the while remaining topless. Her body was Egyptian in its brown color, its even tone, and its proud stance. It was the steam that loosened the towel; its fluffy cotton slipping down against taut flesh, providing a handless, impromptu striptease.

Terri tensed at the memory then whispered back to Derek lustily, "Okay, so you remember when."

Derek looked through her.

"Now what?"

Derek caught her words, winged with sarcasm and desire, the way high brush catches a bird.

Terri watched as his body loosened in submission. He approached with a steely reverence. Terri waited, wanted to feel something, not just sexual, but prime-time, something that would turn the tide or send her floating.

She had missed that kind of feeling. That kind of over-flowing though she was not confused; Terri knew the difference between good sex and a complete fulfilling of body and spirit. But first things first.

I need to know if Derek is still sexy to me, if I still feel a need for his body. Sometimes betrayal can blow up the whole bridge and you don't wanna be bothered with a man period, she reasoned. Everything about him just runs down the drain like so much dirt.

Derek's eyes were moist in the moonlight. He looked down at her, taking in everything about Terri that he loved.

"Your eyes, your mouth, your breasts . . . ," he whispered.

Terri became a sponge and soaked up all the compliments.

She took them for what they were worth—genuine adoration, but she needed more.

Devotion, commitment, trust, Terri thought. Then began chanting in her brain: Can you give them to me?

That's what Terri wished for, but what she got at that moment was hot breath inside her ears and a soft tongue gliding down her collarbone. Derek let her swelled breast fill his mouth like a scoop of ice cream. Terri's insides warmed and she stroked his back.

Derek's movements were sincere, each breath and each touch a sensual sorry. Terri was taking without forgiving; she was reserving all that for instincts yet felt, deeds unseen. But she had decided to entertain the physical begging that she felt in Derek's body.

Beg for me, Terri thought.

And when Derek went to part her legs, Terri locked them at the knees. Derek's eyelids fluttered in surprise.

"Maybe not," Terri said, forcing the words out. She was hot; so hot. But damn if she was going to roll over and play cheap thrill. Beg me, she thought. Then Terri said the words with her eyes.

Derek's soft cry was simply, "Let me kiss you where I miss you."

And Terri smiled then spread herself open like wings.

Chapter 23

Our dreams come to us on wings, either fluttering or soaring.

Grandma Ollie dreamt two dreams that night, one from each variety, both having to do with Terri.

The first dream fluttered into her head. She saw Terri standing in a river with the water up to her knees, but steadily rising. One side was calm while the other side was pitching violently. Terri had no expression on her face, but she clearly seemed to be trying to stay center, not making a move to be completely on one side or the other.

Grandma Ollie felt that she was standing on the riverbank watching Terri, but couldn't see herself. Terri was looking in that direction, frowning like she was puzzled—and the water? It was steadily rising.

When the raging side reached Terri's hip, it surfed up a large wave and crashed high near her chest. Still Terri did not look alarmed. Again the raging side surfed up, but this time the water splashed and reached her collarbone.

Grandma Ollie felt a sensation in her chest, felt like she was yelling, but in the dream she had no voice and no presence. Still Terri seemed to be looking right at her.

It was when the raging side pitched up a third time that it shot up over Terri's head and fashioned a claw that seemed ready to rip her apart.

That's when Grandma Ollie jerked upright in the bed, ending the first dream.

It would take a full hour of deep breaths and single-minded concentration to get Grandma Ollie back in a position to sleep again.

That's when the second dream came soaring.

Grandma Ollie dreamed of her youth. She saw herself sitting in high grass; the blades formed a wall of lushness that cooled the back of her calves. The sound of ten thousand branches whipping the air overhead filled her ears.

Grandma Ollie watched herself, examined her pose, weighed the apprehensive look on her youthful face, then recalled.

This was my blossom time, she thought.

The sound of ten thousand branches whipping overhead became closer and louder. From what Grandma Ollie could tell in the dream, she was sitting up at Lovers Rock.

It was hot, surely summer, as beads of sweat dotted her brow. At this point in the dream Grandma Ollie ceased to be an observer of her post-adolescence early womanhood days and stepped within herself.

She felt a surge of energy that only time bottled up in a dream can give. She felt vibrant again, as if she could jump up and sprint along the water's edge. Instead, her peace was still and the dream continued with only that strange sound.

Thousands of branches: whipping, whipping the wind overhead.

The sound now seemed to overwhelm the sanctity of Lovers Rock. Birds nearby scattered toward the hills; squirrels bolted across the bulging tree roots.

She looked up at the hot sun, and when she did, nature dropped a golden veil over her eyes. Moments later a shower of red began to cut through the haze. As each drop grew closer, it became fuller in size yet soft. The wisps of red wafted down on young Ollie, caressing her skin and uplifting her heart so courageously that she began to laugh out loud.

Grandma Ollie smiled at the sound of her own voice in the dream and thanked God that he had allowed her to remember the sign. Now she knew how to help Terri and save her a third and final time from the river. All Grandma Ollie had to do, she now realized, was to tell Terri about the time rose petals fell from the sky.

Meanwhile Lynnwood was spending his fretful night looking for a way—a way to win Terri over for good. He looked around his modest ranch home, left to him by his parents. His father was a farmer. His mother was a country schoolteacher. There wasn't anything in the house that hadn't belonged to his parents except the weights and the rodeo trophies in the rear room. He compared this with what he imagined Terri had.

Terri owned one of those fancy condos near the lake in

Chicago, her grandmother had bragged. Lynnwood had been through the city once, going to Wisconsin for a rodeo. He envisioned the skyscrapers and thought how hard they looked against the azure blue sky; and how trapped he felt standing in the middle of them, a speck of flesh among mountains of steel.

In some places the buildings were packed in so dense, there was total shade all day despite a brilliant summer sun. At the time, he had felt sorry for the people living there. Now, realizing that that was where Terri might return for good, he felt sorry for himself.

Sometimes from self-pity there rises a phoenix. That was the case for Lynnwood, who was really getting down on himself, tripping on the fact that he made only twenty-two thousand dollars a year and the only thing he owned was this house his parents left him and his truck, and that wasn't worth much.

How little the world values humor and heart; if those two were upheld, Lynnwood would always be the dude that Cinderella married.

So tonight he wondered about romance and things that make today's charmed princesses weak in the knees. How could he win Terri over? Hadn't he shown her the beauty of the quiet around her in Collingswood? Hadn't he shown her the luxury of peace of mind?

But there was evidence for Lynnwood to analyze, a path for him to follow, precedents for him to uphold, shoulders for him to stand on so he might see where to go.

The realization hit Lynnwood and nearly knocked him off

his feet. He stood and ran to the rear closet and pulled out his parents' old treasure chest. It was filled with the things that had made them, them: a baseball glove that Lynnwood's father used during one season barnstorming in the Negro leagues and a box of his handmade fishing lures; an album of pressed flowers his mother put together when she was ten and a quilt made out of Lynnwood's baby things.

Among these treasured items were the most precious things of all. Lynnwood found the locket and a love letter that his father had given to his mother. Lynnwood read the letter again, and within the words composed nearly half a century ago, he finally saw what to do and visualized victory.

And while Lynnwood envisioned that triumph, dreamed of it all night long, and thought of it the next day too, Terri would begin her morning back at Grandma Ollie's house, staring at her Aladdin's lamp and remembering her wish from days before. The thought of that wish now filled her mind and boosted her hope.

Terri had not wished for happiness. She had not wished for wealth. She hadn't even wished for love. Terri had wished for the courage to act.

In her heart, you see, Terri knew that there were times when she knew exactly what direction to go in; there would be no wondering, but what was missing was the courage. Terri wanted the courage that Grandma Ollie had. If only it had been passed down like the family traits of broad noses and loving hats. That would have been so down, so cool, so very righteous.

Instead Terri had inherited only the instinct and was being

forced to develop the straightforwardness needed to act. In short: courage. *Courage* is a word that sometimes is thrown around so lightly you'd think it was a feather. But real courage doesn't float. It anchors.

That was Terri's wish.

As she sat on the couch, glancing out the window at the emerging sun, she wondered if her Aladdin's lamp would work.

Terri was thinking and feeling so hard that she didn't even hear Grandma Ollie roll up behind her in the wheelchair.

"What's wrong, chile?"

Terri turned her head slightly. "Nothing, Grandma Ollie. I'm just thinking."

"Don't think so much sometimes, chile. Just feel."

Sounds like Lynnwood, Terri thought.

"Know what you want and go after it, chile."

Sounds like Derek now, Terri thought.

"Did I ever tell you about your Granddaddy Wesley and the time rose petals fell from the sky?"

Rose petals falling from the sky, Terri thought. "Rose petals?"

Terri turned her body before craning her neck upward. Grandma Ollie's smile was so bright it could be seen clearly in the natural haze of light glowing inside the room. "I'm listening."

"I talk better when a comb and brush figure into the equation," Grandma Ollie said, and cut her eyes at Terri.

That made her laugh. It was a response of quick, sheer joy that came up from the gut. And Terri hopped up, made her way to the bathroom, and grabbed the comb and brush off the lavender vanity table there.

She hadn't heard that saying in years. *I talk better when a comb and brush figure into the equation.*

When Terri and Grandma Ollie would be at odds during Terri's teenage years, they could reason with each other only during a scalp oiling.

It seemed like such a simple thing. Terri would get a stool and begin to comb Grandma Ollie's hair. Then they would share what was on their hearts—woman to woman.

Was it something about the warm, nurturing feeling of someone working oil into the soil of your brain? Or was it because their roles were reversed then, with Terri being the firm one, the caretaker grabbing the lead?

Terri fetched the stool out of the kitchen. It was like a marker, a gauge. When she was a little girl her feet swung high and carefree around the top rung. When she became a teenager, her legs were planted firmly with a cockiness that only brash youth can put down. Now as a woman, she eased up on the stool, placing each foot carefully on a separate rung, and waited; waited for this special time.

Terri took the edge of the comb and pulled it easily through Grandma Ollie's thinning, reddish gray hair. It felt like cotton against her fingertips as she began to create row after row.

Through touch she and Grandma Ollie connected. Through a remembrance she and Grandma Ollie's bond would become even closer.

"Okay, tell me now about how rose petals managed to fall from the sky."

Chapter 24

Near the end of World War II, Collingswood, Arkansas, seemed too big for its britches. There was a big factory that made parts for trucks and a hangar where small military planes were repaired. It seemed as if the town would bust with all the new folk pouring in from even smaller spots and places, taking factory jobs or joining the military.

Ollie made a living at a diner near the factory. Her father rented the building from a wealthy white landowner and hired two friends to cook. Ollie waited tables, and with a quick wit and a flair for flashy scarves draped around her neck, she won a rep for style that put some sho 'nuff copper tips in her apron. She hoped to save enough money to go to nursing school, and then travel. Ollie longed to see the world she could only glimpse once a month at the picture show in a darkened theater two towns over.

But it was a fly guy—literally—that would eventually make Ollie leave the nest and head north to what would become her universe.

The fly guy strutted gallantly with his head held high and his arms thrown back. His uniform hung on him like Greek goddesses had stitched it right on his back with thread spun in the heavens. Muscles puckered the uniform's sleeves and a fine form filled out the back of the trousers. He was *then* what the army was bragging about nearly fifty years later: *Be all that you can be!* When this mystery military man plopped down at the corner table all by his lonesome, Ollie took a stealth survey around the diner's perimeter. She even peeked outside at his jeep, looking for the colored women who surely must have been running behind trying to keep up with this good-looking colored man.

Not since Hank had anyone stopped her in her stance.

"You gonna wait on me, gal, or let me starve to death?" he asked.

That's how their relationship began—with questions. Only it was Ollie who was always doing the asking. She had to ask him his name, Wesley Strong, and where was he from? Alabama. And how long had he been in the service? Since the start of the war. And what did he do? Fly.

Wesley Strong had been in training to be a Tuskegee Airman. But he'd been injured by a swirl of debris that damaged his left eye. Wesley could still see, but his vision was no longer A-one, and that was enough to get him put out of the flying pool. His record was stellar and his attitude top-shelf, so Wesley was allowed to remain in the military.

That's what had brought him to Collingswood, steady work as a repairman on the planes sent over from the nearby base.

What Ollie saw in Wesley was a strong stillness. He seemed so comfortable with himself. But it was not arrogance.

She thought, Boy, you feel so good being you. Here I am some days wondering what I want to do and where I want to be. And you, you some content man in those shoes you walking in, in that space you filling up. There's nothing scary or wishy-washy about you.

Ollie's father liked him. It was the first time he came right out and said he liked one of Ollie's suitors.

"That's a good man there."

"Oh?" Ollie said, faking like she wasn't wondering one way or another. "Do tell."

Ollie's father cut his eyes at her. "Please, Ollie Mae. Save the womanly wiles for Wesley."

"Is it that obvious, Daddy?"

"Just a smidgen. Could only tell because you run in the back when you see him coming and comb ya hair and straighten ya clothes. You give him a double helping of hocks and collards for a single price."

Ollie fell forward and laughed softly into her father's chest. "Aww shoot, Daddy. And here I thought I was baiting the hook before the fish came."

"He knows it. And that's why I like him. Wesley likes you too; but he just don't show it."

And that was the problem.

Wesley took the strong silent type image too far for Ollie's taste. She'd invite him to supper at her house and cook him a wonderful meal, special for him, and he'd say, "Thank you very much." It was so emotionless she halfway expected a tip like they were at the diner.

Wesley would hold her hand as they sat on the porch, but only after Ollie had grabbed his hand first. He'd hug her and Ollie would feel an electric current run through their bodies. But she had to fake a trip and let him catch her first.

"Look, Wesley, I want a respectful man. Sure. But I don't want one in a coma."

"What you talking about, Ollie? I wouldn't think about looking at another woman in this county. Besides the military, I spend all my time with you."

It wasn't a sweet nothing and it wasn't whispered, but it was a declaration of something. So Ollie closed her eyes and let her head fall back gently. She waited anxiously for a passionate kiss. When Ollie opened her eyes, Wesley was looking at her quizzically.

"I thought you were resting your eyes or something," he said in a deadpan voice.

"Naw," Ollie shot back just as deadpan, "I thought you might wanna kiss me or something like that."

Wesley shrugged then he contentedly leaned over and pecked Ollie twice on the cheek.

"You are the most unromantic, mule-headed man I've ever laid eyes on."

Wesley grabbed for Ollie as she stood up and began to stomp away. "Wait a minute, girl."

"Wait for what? A halfhearted kiss? I've seen a rooster

give a hen a better peck than you just gave me. Wait? For what? We've been keeping time for more than six months and you haven't said how you feel about me. So what, you're keeping time with me. A prisoner keeps time with a jail guard too."

"Hold on. Hold on."

"Hold on to what, Wesley? You don't show me a speck of romance. How do I know how you feel?"

"You know how I feel about you, Ollie, don't stand there and tell that lie that you don't."

"How I know, Wesley?"

"Well, everybody around here say you read signs. Can't ya tell?"

"I read signs not minds, hear? And I don't want a mystery man. I want a lover man. And if you can't show me flat-out that I'm the one for you, then get off my porch. Matter of fact get out of my life!"

Wesley reared up and seemed to be a full inch taller.

Oh Lord, what have I've done? Ollie thought. Don't back down now, girl. Hold your position. Hold it.

"If that's the way you want it, fine." And then Wesley walked away. The dust kicked up a storm around his heels because his step was so hard and so earnest.

Unleashed anger will put the heart in a sorrowful place. Ollie looked for Wesley the next day, looked for him to come into the diner for supper. The only sign of him was the dust that an occasional truck kicked up in the road, and that put Ollie in mind of how Wesley would drive fast as he could to get to the diner so he could stay as long as possible, pretending to eat slow but stealing glances at her with a savor similar to thirsty lips sipping good coffee.

Ollie didn't fret that first day he went missing. My God, she thought, the man has to have pride, don't he? Wouldn't want him if he came tail tucked home that fast, would I? Course not.

The second day a line of worry crossed Ollie's brow the way rabbits cross the river, *cautiously*. And she spent the early part of the afternoon cutting her eyes at the door, half expecting to see Wesley lumber in at his regular time.

When a week had passed and Wesley was nowhere to be seen, her girlfriends started to give advice, or rather dip into her business the way a bucket dips deep into a well.

"Ollie, you oughta go to the church picnic with Luther. He's been asking about you like there's no tomorrow. Wesley ain't nowhere to be found. But if he comes to the church picnic it'd be good for him to see that you got more than just his eye."

So Ollie had told Luther, a good-looking, hardworking man around twenty years old, with a job in the factory, that she would make them their box lunch. And there was nothing wrong with Luther. He was all right. But Ollie didn't feel her heart flutter when she saw him or thought about him at night like she did with Wesley.

And that prompting advice and the fact that Wesley had not been to her house or the diner in ten days had Ollie near 'bout in tears. She fought back those tears one night sitting by her open window glancing up at the stars.

Wish I were a star, she thought. They always on the bright side and don't never seem to get lonely.

A tear, solitary only in the path it cut down Ollie's cheek, was quickly wiped away with the back of her hand. Ollie could be stubborn; got that from her mama, her father complained from time to time. She wasn't going to cry her guts out over this man. No sir. Not like she had done for Hank. Those days were good and gone. But if her mind was turning to stone, her heart was still turning to mush.

Ain't nothing like the real thing, baby, the real thing being love. And the way Ollie wanted it and feared that she would never get it was beginning to hurt her deeply. At night sometimes she would glance at an old photo of her mother on Easter Sunday, two years before Ollie was born.

The looming bright yellow hat rivaled the sun that was setting softly just over her shoulder. She had a parasol, posing like she was the grand lady of some Arkansas plantation instead of the seamstress and cook that she was.

Her mother's friends took great pains to nurture Ollie—sharing with her cherished moments they had had with her mother. Ollie almost felt as if she and her mother had shared real conversations, instead of the imaginary ones on nights like these.

"Mama," Ollie spoke to the picture as if it were flesh and blood. "I want a family so bad. But I can't be like Janie and Lula Mae and jump the first horse that comes down the path just 'cause it happen to be going my way."

The photo was the best listener in the world.

"I want somebody who will love me and be good to me. I want someone to do something special for me to show me that he really cares deep down inside. What's wrong about that? Wesley is a good man, Mama, even Daddy thinks so. But I can't give him my heart to hold and he gives me a grunt in return. What kind of life would that be?"

Ollie reached out and clutched the photo.

"How was Daddy with you? I wonder. Quiet, sure. But he had to do something to win your heart, didn't he? Everybody say we have that kindheartedness alike. I get that from you. Why can't I find someone to give to and get something sweet in return? I can't be the one doing all the caring, all the petting, all the loving, all the catering—that ain't right. And won't never be right 'cause time will sho as you born turn it into rust, because I'll get all disgusted."

Ollie drew the picture closer and gazed into her mother's eyes.

"Mama, I always felt you'd watch over me in times of trouble; that you'd be a help to the helpless. Well, that's me, your baby girl Ollie, right about now. I love Wesley with his deep and silent ways but I can't go forth, uh-naw. I can't move not knowing for true and good that Wesley feels the same way about me. Help me, Mama. Help me see the sign that'll let me know for sure. And do, ma'am, right soon. God, how I wish I knew for true that you hear me. I'm just gonna have faith is all."

Ollie drew the photo to her chest and held it there; her heartbeat was so thunderous that it sounded like a storm was opening up outside instead of the steady, silent night.

Ollie clutched and hoped; hoped herself to sleep that night, awaking to the sunrise and the tight pressing of the glass frame against her cheek.

Clearing the sleep from her eyes, Ollie pinched and rubbed them until she saw stars. And with the hazy yolk sliding across the sky near the speckled blue and white clouds, a bird lighted on the windowsill. It was a beautiful bird. A red-beaked, white-feathered bird.

Oh my God, Ollie thought, and reached out to touch it. The bird turned its head and glanced right at her. And just as Ollie's hand touched the back of the bird's tail, it flitted and flew away, but not before looping by the window twice and dropping a feather that wafted down.

Ollie caught it in the palm of her hand and it felt like a kiss from heaven. She closed the feather in her fist and sighed. "Thanks for listening, Mama."

Now, that was the sign that she had been heard. The next sign would be Ollie's answer.

Chapter 25

And that answer would literally fall from the sky.

The church picnic was held after services, in an open field where the brush had been beat back with sickles and the flowers allowed to grow wild. It was a vast space, big enough for picnic tables and an area to play baseball and then some. It was near a brook with thick waters that gurgled against speckled stones as they gushed down a path that would slowly feed deep into the riverbed.

The day of the church picnic the Arkansas sun settled itself above the world like an old storyteller holds court at the general store.

Brilliant and comfortably warm, it was a day that seemed to be watercolored by angels. Each aspect of nature was ample and unrivaled; each speck of cloud, each whisper of wind, each jolly murmur by the parishioners only enriched the day, until folks felt an abundance of joy.

Ollie was terribly alone, in the sense that hers was the only heart falling remarkably short of contentment. Oh, she had made a bountiful, lip-smacking, pound-putting-on-ya-hips box lunch. No doubt. And her wanna-be beau Luther? He came wearing a real hungry look along with his good white shirt and his best tie. But Ollie had no appetite for her fabulously fried green tomatoes, homemade rolls, and braised short ribs. She had no appetite for faked fortunes of the heart. Ollie desperately hungered for Wesley and openly wondered what would become of things. And in her wondering came the realization that she had to do the best thing for all concerned by telling Luther the God's honest truth.

"See, Luther, I was fixing to have lunch with you just because Wesley's not here. And I know in my heart that that is no way to act because you looking for this meal to be the start of something more. And it won't be, Luther. Through no fault or shortcomings of your own at all, it just won't be. That's the truth on the table. It's me, Luther, me that's the wishy-washy one. I'm the one that's stuck on one fellah and can't get outta the mud. So there's no sense in getting a bystander like you dirty for nothing."

Listening with an open mind, Luther fixed his mouth to jaw out a fierce protest. But it was Ollie's eyes that put the period at the end of the conversation. What we see with our own eyes sometimes is a million times more convincing than anything we hear. So Luther was a good man about it; he went on—sad and reluctantly, but he went on just the same.

Ollie wasn't about to send the man away hungry and downhearted, so she gave him the lunch she had prepared and went off by herself.

What Ollie would learn next that day was a fact that would hold her in good stead throughout life: People can surprise you, and people you love can shock the stew out of you.

Wesley was a man of few words and powerful actions.

Ollie was squatting by the brook bank, dipping her hand so she could sip some of the chilly water. She took a trickle and poured it down the space between her cotton dress and her neck. Ollie shivered as the coolness bumped against her shoulder blades and Ping-Ponged all down her back. She closed her eyes and wasn't quite as sad, relishing the cool feeling on her back and the church folks' warm laughter in her ears.

Then Ollie heard this noise. It sounded like branches whipping the wind. It grew nearer and nearer. Ollie opened her eyes and looked up at the sky. She rested the back of her hand against her forehead, palm out to shield her from the brunt of the sun.

She saw a speck lumbering across the sky. It was an old crop-dusting plane.

"Ain't no crops around here," Ollie whispered to herself. She glanced back at where the church folks were picnicking and they too were scrutinizing the sky.

As the plane began flying lower and lower, the sound became more and more thunderous, reminding her of ten thousand branches whipping the sky.

The plane kept getting lower and lower as it circled. Might

crash, mightn't it? Ollie thought. Her heart was beating frantically but she couldn't move. Then the plane did a loop and circled right overhead where Ollie sat. The crop duster flipped upside down and all these little flecks came spilling out.

As they got closer and closer, the red color seemed as brilliant as fire, as if the sky were dropping burning embers.

Ollie ducked her head as the flecks reached her, falling all on her head, her legs, her feet, and in the grass around her. She scooped up some of them. They were soft and silky to the hand, ruby rich to the eye.

"Rose petals," Ollie said aloud. Then she thought, Rose petals falling from the sky.

Then the plane came swooping overhead, pitching and rolling toward a perfect landing in the middle of the baseball field.

The pilot got out and Ollie looked, then looked again. It was Wesley.

The sight of him climbing out of that crop duster made Ollie catch her breath and hold on for dear life. He never glanced anywhere but in Ollie's direction as he came striding toward her.

The church folks had their say as they fell in step right behind him.

"Man, that was some flying, boy!"

"Negro, is you crazy? We thought that plane was 'bout to crash down on our heads!"

The closer Wesley got, the closer Ollie brought the batch of rose petals to her face. She inhaled the smell of them while adoring the sight of him.

"Woman," he said, coming to a halt, and all the folks behind too, like they were a drill team and Wesley was the commander, *and yes he was in command*. "Don't ever make me that mad again. I done brought you flowers. I love you. And I want you to be my wife. Now whatcha gonna do?"

Ollie was dumbstruck with joy. Her tongue froze in place as her brain gave it too many words to say about the love she was feeling right at that moment.

"Shoot," one of the elders in the Queen Easter club crowed, "if'n she won't marry you—I will!"

And the crowd burst out in laughter.

Through that laughter, through that pure joy that her friends and family openly expressed, through that sound, the traffic jam in her brain found its road to freedom. Ollie's emancipated voice ruptured from her throat in two exhilarating shouts of "Yes! Yes!"

She stretched out her arms and Wesley grabbed her up, sweeping her off her feet. Ollie kissed him passionately and Wesley blushed. "Woman, your daddy's over there."

"Oops!"

"Oops what?" Ollie's father joked. "I'm the one told him it was okay. And I'm the one told the boy that you'd be wearing that yallar dress. Ollie Mae, you a grown woman now and you're gonna have your own house to run as you see fit." Then he looked at Wesley seriously. "A house right up the road. Wesley gives me his word he won't take you no further than that. And I'm gonna hold him to it."

All Ollie was trying to hold on to was Wesley. And she did, as tightly as she could. It was one of the happiest days of her life.

Wesley snuggled his face next to Ollie's as he held her close; then he whispered something important in her ear. It was something that had remained just betwixt the two of them for more than fifty years.

Chapter 26

"What did he say, Grandma Ollie?"

"That's for grown folks' ears. You grown?"

"Sometimes it doesn't feel like it, but I've got every grown-folk headache there is—mortgage payments, car payments, job drama, man problems—doggone it, Grandma, I must be grown."

Terri's freewheeling cackle registered soprano, and Grandma Ollie's chuckle was a gritty alto. Together the two women's shared laughter was sweet harmony.

"All right, chile, I'll tell ya what I never told another soul walking this earth in shoes. Wesley whispered, 'Never forget: The deepest fire makes the strongest metal.' "

"What did he mean by that?"

Grandma Ollie sighed, the memory having left her with a toasty feeling deep inside her soul. "He meant that the best love, the one that will last, is deep down simmering and not always flaring up and being real showy. Us knowing that one thing together is what held our marriage up in a righteous manner for more than fifty years. The deepest fire makes the strongest metal."

Then Grandma Ollie made the demonstrative move of leaning forward in her wheelchair and tilting her head at Terri, cutting her eyes. "Hear what I'm saying, girl?"

Terri nodded. Grandma Ollie turned back around and leaned back, real glad and satisfied. Terri began the fifty brush strokes of Grandma Ollie's hair. The ritual had been passed down from generation to generation; a sharing of thoughts while oiling one's scalp, then a hard brushing of fifty strokes to settle the hair and the shared experience.

Terri used the slow repetition of movement to think, to think about the night she had just spent with Derek. Their lovemaking had relit a doused flame. She'd felt satisfied, even passionately rejuvenated.

What did all this mean? She and Derek still clicked physically. But so what? Could they move forward? Was it worth a try? What about Lynnwood?

Terri and Lynnwood had not had sex; they clicked on an entirely different level. She felt safe with Lynnwood, felt like she was sharing time with, say, a part of herself—no, no, that thought felt way too strong. It was, wasn't it? What was the real deal?

The deal was more like Lynnwood could be with you and you know it, then not know it. Effortless would be the very best way to describe it. His presence to Terri was effortless and comfortable.

Maybe Lynnwood would just be a good friend. Maybe that was the shape their relationship was meant to take in the universe. I mean, Terri thought, if they did hook up and try to have a relationship, what were they going to do, fly back and forth? She'd be coming down to Collingswood anyway from time to time to see about Grandma Ollie. But Terri had been in long-distance romances before and they were just hateful. You ended up spending a ton of money and the glow seemed to wear off awful quick—last time she'd been out a few grand in plane fare before even racking up enough frequent flyer miles to get a free ticket.

Would it be a waste of time? A waste of emotion?

Terri waffled her options: Lynnwood could just be a good friend. They were two different people with different wants and desires. He'd never be comfortable in the big city with her and the political career she envisioned. And there was nothing for her here in the small town of Collingswood.

Terri made a mental note to hook up with Lynnwood as soon as possible to clear up the situation. Why let things fester? As much as Grandma Ollie was pulling for Lynnwood, it just didn't seem like it would work in Terri's mind, or could it? She leaned down now and kissed the old woman on the cheek. "Finished and don't you look fine, girl."

"Looked fine before you commenced, now I'm really slamming."

Terri's mouth dropped. Then she tapped the comb against Grandma Ollie's shoulders. "Where'd you learn that?"

"I got eyes and ears," she said, rolling the wheelchair away from Terri, rotating it around to face her. "You know your cousin can't clean a house unless she's got those BET videos playing on the TV."

"Ain't that the truth, Grandma Ollie."

"Chile, when I was young, black entertainment was Sammy Davis Jr. and Lena Horne. Not shake ya fast."

The two women shared another laugh and only became distracted by the cowbell clang of the front door.

"Speak of the devil."

"Yep," Terri said, heading for the door, "you've talked Sugar up. She should have been here a half hour ago."

Standing at the front door was Derek, holding a big round box with a cream-colored bow on top. He motioned with his head toward the living room and mouthed the name, *Grandma Ollie.*

Terri smiled and admonished herself on the inside, Stop grinning at him so, fool. The smile slowly slid off her face. "C'mon in."

Derek had on a pair of navy blue slacks and a royal blue muscle shirt that exploited his mountainous body, with its Rushmore abs and Kilimanjaro shoulders. He scooted around the corner setting the pretty box on the tabletop in the living room where Grandma Ollie sat.

"Hey, lovely lady."

"Hey back. That's a pretty box you got there, boy."

Derek walked over to Grandma Ollie with a swagger, then knelt down. "It's for you."

"A surprise?" Grandma Ollie asked, her face flushing a warm color as the corners of her mouth curled up into a smile.

"Yes. Go over there and put it on. The mirror is right there."

Terri walked up and stood next to Derek. They both

watched as Grandma Ollie unwrapped the bow and pried open the box. "Lookah here." Slowly she pulled out a wide-brim hat made of embroidered lace with a satin border tied in a bow on the side. It was a rich cream color. "I'll be the Mad Hatter for sure in this beauty."

Grandma Ollie's pinky fingers jetted out like wings as she navigated the hat on top of her head. Derek closed the short distance between him and this dapper old lady with a marked swagger. Now he and Grandma Ollie took up the entire space in the oval wall mirror.

"See? Thought you said a leopard can't change its spots?"

"Can't," Grandma Ollie said, cocking the hat flush left, "but yours are definitely getting smaller. That's the truth."

Derek kissed her on the cheek. "You're a hard lady."

"Boy, how you think I've lived so long?"

Outside Sugar did her shimmy walk up the driveway, creeping, just like the backup singers croon on that Luther Vandross record, *creep-creep-creep.*

She stopped two feet away from the man's back. "Whatcha lookin' at, Boo?"

Lynnwood nearly left the skin he was born in. He jerked up, and sighed. "Sugar, you sneak. That was dirty."

"Me? You're the Peeping Tom. What? You so sweet on my cuz that you gotta stare her down through the window before you buck up enough courage to ring the bell?"

Before Lynnwood could answer, Sugar piped up in an off-key loud *I think I'm jamming* voice, "Sho 'nuff must be love!"

Lynnwood leapt forward and covered her mouth. Sugar's chest heaved as she laughed. He slid his hand down.

"It's got to be—"

Lynnwood slapped his palm back over her mouth. "C'mon. Who you for, a country boy like me or that city cat in there?"

Sugar stopped laughing, then frowned. She sauntered over to the window and took a peek. "I can't stand that nickel-slick joker and that's real."

"Thanks, Sugar. At least I have somebody on my side for sure. The two of them are flip-flopping like hooked catfish. One minute they talking about Derek then the next minute— well, see there, you got eyes. Terri's grinning and Grandma Ollie was grinning too. He's a tough guy to compete with."

"C'mon, Lynnwood. Are you gonna let that city boy bamboozle you? If you do, you ain't no friend of mine. Don't punk out . . . I mean, you're one of the nicest guys around. All he's got is style, money, a big-time job . . ."

"Sugar, don't help me. Help the bear."

"You know what I'm saying. He's shallow stuff; you got substance on your side."

"And," Lynnwood held up a yellowed envelope, "history."

"What's that?" Sugar asked.

"The key to me winning your cousin's heart and sending Derek's weak ass back to the Windy City."

Sugar high-fived Lynnwood. "Get down, boy. That's what I'm talking about. Don't get scared. Get down."

"I've got a plan, Sugar. Will you help me?"

"Do chitterlings come from a pig? What do I have to do?"

"Just get Terri to the rodeo. That woman is gonna know how I feel about her if I gotta die trying."

Chapter 27

Lynnwood hovered above a killer.

Directly below him the hairy, humpbacked bull snorted and kicked; sheer murder choreographed his every move.

Lynnwood reached down and grabbed the braid with his thick, gloved hand and braced the sides of the wooden shoot with his heels.

The bull had killed one man before.

That cowboy had tried to ride him last year. The bull threw him so hard his breastbone cracked and a piece staked right through the cowboy's heart.

Lynnwood's heart was on the line today too, not just his hide.

He searched and found Terri sitting in the stands. The crowd paled around her as if she were an angel of love and they were just trying to get close to the gate.

"You liable to kill yourself, Wood," one of the cowboys said in a scalding voice. "And for what? You're a bronco rider not a bull rider. Brother, this bull is the toughest one going for miles around. Why don't you forget about it?"

Lynnwood wasn't having it. Every year for the last sixty years there was prize money for whoever stayed the longest on the most notorious bull in Arkansas County. It was an honored tradition in those parts.

Not only did the winner bank some big bucks; he also got to make a little speech to the crowd. That's what Lynnwood was really after. That's what he held in the highest esteem.

"I'm riding," he said. "I'm doing this, man."

"Well then," one of the older, grizzled cowboys advised, "keep your concentration. Especially when you want to dismount, Wood. Broken concentration makes for some broke bones."

"What else?"

"Keep a thought, something simple, that'll help with your concentration. Always did for me, boy, and I won this thing twice in my youth. But it wasn't in front of a whole bunch people like it is now. That's for sure."

The Collingswood Rodeo drew more than three thousand people from nearby counties and the surrounding states. It was the biggest thing held in the small town besides the Summer Social.

Circular wood planks enclosed the ring where the state's best cowboys would compete for top prizes in broncobusting, roping, bulldogging, and other events.

The shoots that held the bulls were narrow, with no slits

for light. The bulls and broncos hadn't been fed since the day before, to keep them in an ornery mood.

All the cowboys had on their best hats, big looping ten-gallon toppers like Hoss's from *Bonanza,* or dainty bad black boys that they cocked to the side like Little Joe.

Lynnwood had opted for the Little Joe style. He gazed down at the bull scratching and clawing at the densely packed dirt and straw floor. The bull's bloated sides scraped the walls of the shoot, causing fine splinters to fly. Lynnwood held the braid and braced the walls of the shoot with his heels, waiting for the right moment to drop down on the bull's back and fling his arm upward, the signal to open the door.

The bull herking and jerking below him began to represent the unbridled things in Lynnwood's life. The way he'd lost his mother and father within a matter of months of each other; his father to skin cancer, his mother to a broken heart.

The way he'd dropped out of the workforce, leaving his high-profile job as a county manager in the state's social services office, spending all his savings as he mourned and zoned at his parents' home, too distraught to pack up their clothes or change the property over into his name until last year.

The way he thought he was content, taking a low-profile job reading to the sick, thinking the attention and affection he showed them was enough to anchor his soul.

But all that was just smoked honey.

The sweetness of it all masked beneath it a smoldering desire to get back into the world and fight for something, or someone.

Terri had gotten under Lynnwood's skin and had become the billowing power that stoked his smoldering desire. The momentum rose and rose almost endlessly, until it had filled Lynnwood's veins, bursting them from the inside out, sending that stream of smoked honey crashing through the blood until it became a puddle bubbling around his unfulfilled heart.

Lynnwood was the last rider. Only three had even dared. The record to beat was seventeen seconds. He needed to do better than that to win a chance at Terri's love. Lynnwood gazed up into the stands at what he considered the real prize, and instead caught a glimpse of the enemy.

Derek was bungling his way through the seated crowd until he found a spot and managed to squeeze right next to Terri. "This place smells like shit and I'm stepping in shit." He peeked at his Stacy Adams shoes. "These loafers cost a hundred dollars. Good thing I didn't wear my Jordans."

"Yeah, yeah," Sugar said in a high, snarled voice. Then she bent down and shot a piercing look at him. "What you doing here?"

"I've been trying to find y'all all afternoon. It's a good thing I saw the note you left on the table for Grandma Ollie."

"As I recall, *your* name was nowhere on that note. It said 'Dear Grandma Ollie . . .' "

Derek shrugged, "She had just woke up and couldn't find her reading glasses, so I helped her out. So what? Get off my case." Derek was getting real tired of Sugar and her crooked mouth; she was always messing with him. "Bitch. Bitch. Moan. Moan."

Sugar popped up, her hands saddling her bountiful hips. "Who are you calling a bitch?"

Terri yanked Sugar down by the arm. "That's not what Derek meant and you know it, girl. Sit your humbugging tail down right now."

Derek hissed out a mean little chuckle.

"And you, mister, put that hot tongue on ice or I'm gonna make it my business to take both of you down a few pegs."

Sugar and Derek were silent, but each managed to murder the other with a machete stare.

Terri threw her hands up around her eyes like blinders, blocking Sugar and Derek's view of each other. That forced him to glance down at one of the stalls. "Hey, isn't that the guy who reads to Grandma Ollie down there? Don't tell me he's about to ride that bull."

Sugar snorted. "Yeah, he is. And Lynnwood ain't scared and he ain't worried about getting his shoes dirty."

"He needs to be worried about breaking his behind," Derek shot back sarcastically. "That bull looks dangerous. He's a fool to try a stunt like that just to win some chump change."

"Don't talk about Lynnwood like that." Terri jerked around. And she was surprised by her upbraiding tone.

So too was Derek. "Are you snapping at me, Terri?"

Terri didn't answer the question and didn't back off her tough tone. "Lynnwood is a different kind of man is all. Don't dog him, Derek, cheer for him."

Derek shrugged rather reluctantly, "Okay. Okay. Sorry."

Sugar leaned back and stuck her tongue out at Derek, "Ahhha!"

Terri threw an elbow at Sugar.

"Ouch," Sugar grunted.

"Stop picking on Derek, I mean it."

"Thanks for the backup, baby," Derek said, snuggling with Terri, rubbing it in extra well for Sugar's benefit.

From the rodeo pit, Lynnwood watched as Derek hugged Terri, then whispered in her ear before giving her a kiss. That sight was like spurs to his hide.

"Yeee-hah!" Lynnwood yelped, dropping down on the bull and throwing up his hand.

The shoot was slow to open so the bull helped it a lot by ramming it with his noggin so hard that it sounded like a gunshot as the door whipped against the side of the corral and the latch flew off into the stands.

"Lord, Lynnwood," Terri said under her breath in a deep, prayerful manner. "Lord."

And with an atomic urgency, the infinite horizon that belongs to everyone melted down to a cocoon of two. In the next few seconds, Terri saw, heard, felt, and cared about no one else but Lynnwood.

She watched his left arm; down, board straight, paralyzed around the braid, gripping it for life everlasting. Lynnwood's loose right arm and the rest of his body jerked around like a stringed puppet with demons at the controls. Terri was so in tune with Lynnwood that she could feel the wrenching and lurching in her own bones as the bull rocked and rolled his body.

A huge time clock in the center of the display board was hoisted high above the stands. The second hand slowly hacked forward, chopping into each interval of time like the sleepy blink of an eye.

"Lord, Lynnwood," Terri whispered into her cupped hands, which rose fitfully to her mouth. "Lord."

His hips arched up as the bull whipped around, causing Lynnwood to slide down the animal's mountainous spine.

The bull's breezy momentum blew Lynnwood's free arm about like a half-pinned shirt hanging off a clothesline.

He tried to steer the animal with his boot heels, shifting his weight to the right as the bull careened toward the left side of the corral fence. But Lynnwood didn't shift fast enough. His right arm flopped down and the edge of his hand scraped the top rung of the corral.

"Ohhh!" the crowd gasped.

Lynnwood began to skid sideways, headed for the belly of the bull, his head now swaying several inches above the ground.

A cowboy yelled, "Ride 'im just five more seconds!"

Lynnwood managed to yank himself upright. And the crowd cheered. The bull was working furiously to unseat the burden on his back. He bucked up and down so hard that he managed to lift his body a whole two feet off the ground, including all four hooves.

Lynnwood felt the violent thumping in his breastbone and in the curves of his jaws. He clenched his teeth and lips together so tightly that his saliva jelled in the back of his throat. You couldn't have convinced him before now that a person could feel this much pain in such a short amount of time. Couldn't have convinced him of that.

Now he knew it.

People have heard of catch-22. Lynnwood was now facing the *catch 2 and 2*: Doubt and fatigue plus dismay and failure. Lynnwood began to doubt that he could make it another second longer, because his body was racked with fatigue. That filled him with dismay because failure would cost him the woman he believed to be the love of his life.

Lynnwood's eyes fed him ragged, false images. Blackened chunks of dirt and splinters of scattered straw seemed miles below him. His mind, however, told him that the ground was closer than it looked, just like the manufacturer's warning found on a car's side-view mirror.

The image of the crowd had the clearness and the ripple of water. He searched for that one special set of eyes, that one set whose gaze could inject him with just enough bravado to win.

Lynnwood found Terri's eyes.

She, of course, had been locked in on him the entire time. And remember the horizon had melted and placed their spirits in a cocoon. Lynnwood's sagging spirit focused on Terri. And through all that yelling and screaming, Lynnwood picked out her voice easier than it would have been to pick out a needle in a haystack.

"Hang on!"

Those words gave him the last bit of daring he needed to fight against fate using his hopes for playthings. He struggled to unclench his teeth, to free his voice, sure that at the right moment, Terri would be able to read his lips and his heart.

And when he knew that the impossible was possible, that he had maxed out, that he had beat the best time, Lynnwood took a tremendous chance. It was a chance that would cause him to lose his concentration as he waited for the right split second to dismount the bull safely. Lynnwood gazed at Terri and mouthed two words. The two words he mouthed were the thought he had been advised to keep. The words had provided the steel for his backbone; had been the thump in the beat of his heart.

And those two words were "For you."

Chapter 28

When we can find the courage to do for others what we cannot do for ourselves, life's possibilities will bloom.

Terri intimately felt the words Lynnwood spoke, despite the lengthy distance. She felt them as deeply as if he had been standing right next to her and he had just whispered each word in her ear.

The impact of it all twirled inside her brain. Terri cautiously weighed the powerful connection that had just been solidified between the two of them. She realized that what they had exchanged was special.

And in a split second, what was beautifully extraordinary became challenged by danger.

Lynnwood's steely left hand finally gave way and his body flipped off the bull's back and sailed high in the air. He looked powerless and discarded, aimless and in jeopardy.

Mercifully Terri's memory died.

She did not remember leaving the stands in a fitful dash. She never felt Derek grab her arm or question where she was going and why. Terri didn't remember shaking him off either. She didn't remember blowing past the security officers that at first moved into her path, but seeing her eyes, stepped aside and let her pass.

Terri didn't remember seeing Lynnwood land or the bull dancing dangerously near his head just before the rodeo clowns lured the beast away until he could be caught and caged.

Terri's memory was reborn at Lynnwood's side. He lay unconscious, the crowd holding a collective breath, saying a collective prayer for this man who had just pulled off a valiant ride.

A doctor was kneeling over Lynnwood, locating smelling salts in his bag.

"Is he going to be okay?" Terri asked.

"Wood is tough as nails, lady," one of his cowboy friends said, although the words were more a hope than a statement.

Terri touched his face as the doctor applied the smelling salts. And she was the first person he saw after regaining consciousness. Lynnwood gave her a crooked, pleased-as-all-outdoors smile. "Hey."

Terri took his hand. "Hey back."

The doctor checked Lynnwood's legs and arms. A grimace told everyone that his right wrist was sprained. "You're a lucky man."

Lynnwood didn't avert his gaze from Terri and said simply, "Don't I know it."

"We need to get him to the hospital to run some tests. I want to check for a concussion—just to be safe—but I think he'll be just fine."

As the men around him began to lift him onto a stretcher, Lynnwood squeezed Terri's hand tightly.

Now Derek was stopped cold by security at the entrance of the corral. "But that's my fiancée in there."

The security guard glanced over at Terri and Lynnwood, who were holding hands. "Don't look like it."

Derek stared at them angrily.

Lynnwood asked Terri, "Would you do me a favor?"

"Sure, you know that, what?"

"Accept my prize for me, and read my speech—it's all written down right here. Go in my left shirt pocket."

Terri reached into the pocket and pulled out three rumpled pieces of paper. She gently patted his chest. "Don't worry. I'll read it nice and loud for you."

Lynnwood slowly closed his eyes as they began to carry him away.

"Let him rest," the doctor told Terri as she walked alongside the stretcher.

When they reached the security point where Derek stood trapped, he grabbed Terri by the arm. "What the hell is going on?"

"What?"

"What have you been doing down here all this time," Derek growled, then added with a jerky nod of the head, *"with him?"*

"Nothing, and if I had, I know you're not trying to act indignant, please."

"Did you screw him?"

"Don't talk under my clothes like that!" Terri yelled at him. Everyone was watching them now. "We're friends. And where do you get off cross-examining me anyway, huh?"

"All I'm saying, Terri, is it looked damn cozy out there between the two of you. You're just friends, huh? Please, run
that by somebody with 'stupid' tattooed on his skull. Not me,
baby. Something is up, okay? Let's get out of here; roundup
time is over."

Terri dug in. "I can't. I have to accept Lynnwood's prize
for him and give his speech."

"What? I'm not having that. We're leaving right now!"

Sugar was standing by, watching all the action. As soon as
she heard Derek say he wasn't having it, she went to get a
couple of Lynnwood's cowboy buddies.

"What's got you tripping so hard, Derek, huh?"

"This: You're going to be my wife and I don't like you
kneeling down next to some broke-down Roy Rogers type,
holding his goddamn hand in front of thousands of people.
You're not gonna embarrass me like that, no."

The rodeo manager came over to Terri. "Excuse me, it's
time to accept Lynnwood's prize."

Derek piped up. "She's not available."

"Yes, I am," Terri said, spinning on her heels and walking
away.

Derek went after her.

His path was blocked by a couple of two-by-fours: two big
cowboys with four huge fists cocked and ready. One of them
said, "Wood wanted her to speak for him and that's the way
it's gonna be."

Derek stepped back and threw up his fists too. "Y'all not
gonna make me look like a punk."

"You can look like a punk or you can look like an accident victim," Sugar said from behind him. "Which one is it gonna be?"

Derek weighed his options and dropped his hands in frustration. "Terri!"

She stopped walking, then turned. Terri focused her whole world on Derek at this moment, all their history, all their ups and downs; all of that in zoned focus, as she listened intently with her heart.

"Terri, if you go up there, it's over and I mean it. No fixing it. You go up there and I'm gone on the next plane. I'm not looking back."

Subconsciously Terri had been holding her breath. Didn't know it. Wasn't trying to. She just was. Something left her at that moment, the way color disappears from tree leaves, the way a sweet smell vanishes from the kitchen air, the way tears leave sorrowful eyes, and that way was quick and for good.

Terri turned and walked to the podium. The rodeo manager handed her Lynnwood's check. She took it and got ready to speak on his behalf. Terri stood in front of the microphone, the southern breeze gently patting her back. She swallowed hard, glanced at her cousin Sugar in the wings, and then began to speak clear and strong.

"My name is Terri Mills. They took Lynnwood to the hospital with a sprained wrist but the doctor says he'll be just fine."

The crowd cheered and the golden sound was carried high into the trees by the sweeping winds.

"Lynnwood asked me to accept this prize on his behalf and read the thank-you speech he's written."

Terri paused to unfold the crumpled pieces of paper. The

first page was a half sheet of white paper with cursive writing in pen, followed by a full unlined sheet of brown paper printed in pencil, then another half sheet just like the first. Terri began reading:

"Ladies and gentlemen, my father won this prize forty years ago and he dedicated that victory to a special lady, my mother. This is the letter that he wrote to her then and left under her pillow that night:

My sweet—I thank God for you. Today whenever I got afraid and had my doubts, I thought of you and that made me strong.

The prize they handed out today is nothing when set down next to you. I'm so glad I have you in my life. That's what makes me a winner every single day I live. This glory I have right now I share with you.

So now I follow in my father's footsteps and dedicate this victory to the special lady in my life—TERRI MILLS."

The crowd let out a feel-good moan that resonated in the pit of Terri's stomach. Her reading voice had almost lost steam, falling one octave at a time when she saw that Lynnwood had written her name in big letters and had ended the sentence with a heart. She traced the paper heart with her fingertips. Terri's lips trembled as she folded up the pages and put them next to her own heart. She closed her eyes, then paid him homage before the crowd by leaning into the microphone and saying breathlessly, "Thank you, Lynnwood."

Chapter 29

Breathing room is best measured by the person trying to survive. How much space is needed for breathing room? How much space in the physical state and how much space in the mental state?

Terri had so much happen to her in a fragment of a lifetime that she felt as if her world was encased in a translucent bubble. Her very existence seemed trapped within a boundary that was so fragile that at any moment it could burst and everything that seemed so clear would again turn into scummy bubbles of doubt.

Terri needed breathing room.

She had her heart in the right place and her mind on the right track, but one last thing was needed to confirm to Terri all that she perceived to be possible if life and love could be experienced without any boundaries and with plenty of breathing room.

Terri decided not to go to Derek to say good-bye to him and what they once had. No one need shed tears when a romance dies a natural death. Mourners don't have to shake their heads and whisper about a love lost too soon. That body is dead and buried, no need to pray over it. Everyone must go on with life.

So Terri went on, went on to Lovers Rock, alone. In our solitary time we can confront the limits we put on ourselves and ask God to reenforce what we know in our spirit is limitless.

It was there that Terri sat and remembered: remembered that Grandma Ollie had been here with Hank and Grandpa Wesley. She understood what Grandma Ollie had experienced here and how she had grown here as well.

Terri knew exactly what she wanted to do and needed to have. She wanted to have a relationship with Lynnwood. For it to be blessed Terri needed to go into it with an open mind and an open spirit; and not the tattered covers that she wore so often to protect her thoughts and her heart.

Terri sat and meditated, deciding to let the magic of Lovers Rock do its thing. Magic is like a reflection in rippling water; we can see it taking shape but we can't shape it like we want to.

So Terri waited until she felt tingly all over but not from the cool air that chased behind the setting sun. Terri felt tingly because the more she thought about what she wanted the more determined she was to have it. She wanted it so bad it was a low-down dirty shame. And Terri realized that she didn't want it as much for herself as she did for Lynnwood, who was the best man she had ever known.

And when we can want more for someone else than we want for ourselves, there is a tenderness that can't be tarnished by any worldly mess.

Terri was now ready for love's latest journey. This time she was packed and better prepared than she had ever been before. That's when Terri realized that her wish had come true, the wish that she had made several days before on her childhood Aladdin's lamp. It had come true. She now had courage.

Terri walked down the steep side of Lovers Rock. She didn't stumble or stutter-step. Each move was steady and sure. She found herself at Lynnwood's house just as the sun began to put itself to bed behind the bluish orange cover of the sky.

Lynnwood answered the door wearing just jeans and no shirt, his arm in a sling tied with a knot around his neck that looked like a set of rabbit ears. He gazed at Terri and opened the screen door without a word.

She said nothing, reaching inside, taking him by the good arm and leading him over to the swing on the front porch. Terri sat Lynnwood down and cuddled next to him, letting her head fall safely onto his shoulder. She was as dark and soft as milk chocolate left out in the sun.

Terri said, "Thank you, Lynnwood. Thank you for waiting patiently."

"But now patience has run out," he answered, then kissed her passionately.

They held each other close and sat there quietly watching

the last rays of sun fade away. When it was nearly night, Terri whispered in Lynnwood's ear.

She said, "Never forget: The deepest fire makes the strongest metal."

"I won't forget."

EPILOGUE

The Good Sign

Grandma Ollie let her weight slide down into her double-cushioned chair by the window. That was her usual spot whenever she waited patiently for her ride to Wednesday night prayer meeting. Grandma Ollie yanked and snapped her good white gloves to a creaseless press before laying them on her lap and opening up the family Bible.

The first page read, "Given To:" Her father had written in his fifth-grade hand her name and the date . . .

Olivia Anderson. June 4, 1935.

She turned to the page entitled "Marriages." There, many years ago, she had written herself . . .

Olivia Anderson engaged to Wesley Strong on April 19, 1943.

Beneath that she'd written . . .

Married August 28, 1944, 'til death do them part.

Grandma Ollie paused to reflect.

Theirs had been a simple wedding. Wesley's only request was that there wouldn't be too many people. Two hundred guests were there. *So much for his only request,* which set the tone for most of their lives, because Ollie always managed to have her way and Wesley knowingly allowed it. Ollie wanted to have the ceremony at six in the evening. Odd it seemed to her father and her friends, *oddly sentimental.*

Ollie wore her mother's white satin wedding dress. Her father kept it for his daughter, wrapped in a quilt that his mother had given the couple for a wedding present. The heavy quilt had been like a bridesmaid holding the dress in her lap; the dress was wrinkle free and as pretty as the day it was last worn.

Ollie wanted her wedding in the evening because at that exact time, the setting sun's rays would gleam through the sanctuary windows. The rays would flow past her back in a yellow haze, like they had her mother's in Ollie's favorite picture.

Remembering the wedding now made Grandma Ollie think, The deepest fire makes the strongest metal. We had some of the best times, didn't we, old Wes? We were happy living down here in Collingswood after the war, especially after Magpie was born. I know you hated it when I pushed us to move after Daddy died in his sleep. With him gone and work so scarce, up north seemed the place to be. And didn't it turn out just fine? Even with the bone-cold weather and noisy streets that took you so long to get used to? Didn't we live and love each other just fine? That's why when you passed on, I felt like I had to move, just like when Daddy died. I come back home here to the family house in Collingswood, come back full circle, yes Lord.

Grandma Ollie went to where she had begun to write . . .

Terri Mills engaged to . . .

That's when her pen had run out of ink before, just as she tried to write Derek's name.

Grandma Ollie finished it now. She wrote:

. . . Lynnwood Conway on August 29, 2002.

Grandma Ollie chuckled softly, remembering how nervous that boy looked at the Summer Social in the old military barn. Looked like an overweight turkey on Thanksgiving eve with four guns aimed at him. Sho did. But wasn't it romantic though? That's what Grandma Ollie liked about that boy; he had a flair for romance. And wasn't that a beautiful thing? Told nobody else to dance when that song came on, what was it? "Here and Now," they said, by Luther Vandross.

The two of them had danced alone in front of everyone. Deacon Homer and Grandma Ollie were sitting off to the side eyeballing the entire situation. He kept goosing Grandma Ollie with his elbow. "Lookah there . . . Lookah there."

She had to tell him, "Hush, you old coot!"

Lynnwood proposed, and then gave Terri a locket that his father had given his mother. They would be married next fall.

Grandma Ollie gently closed the Bible and felt infinitely satisfied, satisfied because Terri had found lessons in her life experiences and had used them to guide her to Lynnwood, a true love.

Grandma Ollie pushed off on her pearl-handled "going to church" cane. Her body seemed heavier than usual but her heart was light with happiness. She walked over to the mirror hanging on the wall and picked up her favorite hat off the table. It was the hat that Terri had given her this Mother's Day. It was ruby red with a veiled border that had a satin rose fashioned on the side. Terri said it was to remind her of the time rose petals fell out of the sky.

Grandma Ollie adjusted it just so, with a bit of a tilt to the right and a low-brow drop in the front till she could barely see.

"G'on, girl. You still got it!" she said admiringly to the mirror.

Outside the gravelly road announced the slow approach of a car. It was time to meet her ride. Grandma Ollie made her way to the front door with her cane. She opened the door and the sunshine embraced her entire body. Then a bird sailed softly over her head, chirping a satisfied melody. Grandma Ollie tipped her hat with a nod, acknowledging the spirited flight. "That's a good sign. Lord, it's going to be a beautiful evening."

About the Author

Yolanda Joe is the bestselling author of *He Say, She Say; Bebe's By Golly Wow;* and *This Just In.* Under the pseudonym Ardella Garland, she is also the author of two mysteries. Formerly a television news producer and writer, she is a graduate of Yale and the Columbia School of Journalism and now lives in Chicago.